BECAUSE WE DREAMED

A CHRISTIAN ROMANCE

JULIETTE DUNCAN

TRANSFORMED BY LOVE SERIES - BOOK 3

PRAISE FOR "BECAUSE WE DREAMED"

"This book made me feel along with them. There are important truths woven seamlessly into the book. This is one of my favorite's of Juliette Duncan's works. ~*Lisa*

"This is a book that you don't forget when you read the last page. I love how the author places bible verses through out the story that will lift you up as you read." ~*Ann*

"Ms. Duncan weaves Christian values and scripture into the book in such a meaningful way." ~*Mary*

"What a true to life story! The anguish of Amy and Angus is so realistic. The scripture that encouraged them both has become my new favorite!! The way that God brought them together with Marta was so inspiring! I thoroughly enjoyed this book and can't wait for the next one!" ~*Susan*

"I always look forward to books by this author and this one again lived up to my expectations. A story of sadness joy and hope as a couple come to terms with their loss. I love the way there is gentle teaching threaded throughout. Waiting in anticipation for the next part of this series." ~*Judith*

FOREWORD

HELLO! Thank you for choosing to read this book - I hope you enjoy it! Please note that this story is set in Australia. Australian spelling and terminology have been used and are not typos!

As a thank you for reading this book, I'd like to offer you a FREE GIFT. That's right - my FREE novella, "Hank and Sarah - A Love Story" is available exclusively to my newsletter subscribers. Click here to claim your copy now and to be notified of my future book releases. I hope you enjoy both books! Have a wonderful day!

Juliette

PROLOGUE

*A*ll day Amy knew something was wrong. She woke with a nagging, gnawing pain low in her belly, and her first thought was to put her hand over the area to protect the precious life growing inside her.

She and Angus had waited so long. They'd been trying for a baby for years, and while she'd done her best to be patient and trust that it would happen in God's time, there'd been times when she'd felt as though her hoping was fruitless and she'd wondered if she'd have to accept that having children was not part of God's plan for them at all.

All she'd ever wanted to be was a mother. Gregarious and outgoing, she was the perfect counterbalance to the quiet and steady Angus, the love of her life. Her only love, until the day she'd taken the pregnancy test and joy like nothing else enveloped her. They'd both cried tears of gratitude that night.

As the day wore on, the cramps grew worse, so she left work early and phoned Fleur, her best friend. She and Fleur had been inseparable since high school. Quiet but determined, Fleur had been an inspiration to Amy on many an occasion, not least because of her devoted faith. Fleur had cried on her shoulder when her first husband died in combat, and again, this time with joy, when she married her second just a few weeks earlier. She and Callum had only returned from their honeymoon two days ago.

"What should I do?" Amy asked. "I phoned the doctor, but she told me to take paracetamol and go in tomorrow if the pain continues."

"And did she also say to rest?" Fleur asked pointedly.

Amy groaned and rolled her eyes. "Yes, she told me to rest. Fleur, do you think this is normal?"

Fleur's hesitation gave Amy cause for concern. "I don't remember ever having pain like that with Lucy or Will, but everybody's different. It's probably nothing. Do what the doctor says and take it easy. Would you like me to come over later? I can ask Callum to watch the children."

Amy felt grateful for her friend, but she wanted to be alone, which was unusual. She hadn't yet told Angus her concerns, as if voicing them to him could make her fears real. "I'll be okay, but thanks."

"It's what I'm here for, Amy," Fleur said gently. "Call me if you need me."

Amy put the phone down and went to bed, her hand once again over her stomach. She tried to tell herself everything would be okay. The baby would be here in just under seven months and all would be well. Even Will and Lucy were excited. Amy was the children's godmother and had been there for them all their lives, and they saw her baby as a little brother or sister.

Tired and cold, she pulled an extra blanket over her body as she curled up. She didn't intend to sleep, just rest, but suddenly her lids grew heavy and she felt herself drifting off.

Sometime later she woke to Angus shaking her urgently. "Amy! Amy!"

She sat up. His face was as white as a sheet.

She followed his gaze. That's when she saw the blood...

A FEW DAYS later she sat with Angus in the consultant's office at Salford General, her head on his shoulder. Not just her body, but her soul felt weary. Empty.

The consultant gave her a sympathetic smile which didn't quite reach her eyes. Amy supposed she got used to scenes like this. It must be routine for her, whereas for Amy and Angus, their whole world had suddenly fallen apart.

"The good news," the consultant said gently, "is that there's no lasting damage and no need for any procedures."

"So, we can try again?" Angus asked.

Amy heard the eagerness in his voice, lifted her head and looked at him. He'd spent the past few days tending to her and comforting her without any real mention of how the miscarriage had affected him. She felt as though she was moving through fog and had barely registered her own pain let alone her husband's, but now she realised with a small jolt that he was hurting, too. And as was his pragmatic way, he would want to find a solution.

But did she want to try again? She hadn't even accepted

that this baby was gone. She'd refused to let Angus send any of the baby things back to the shops, although they hadn't bought much as they'd wanted to wait until she was further along. Now she knew why.

She looked at the consultant, waiting for the answer. Her stomach plummeted as the woman frowned and seemed to be searching for the right words. "You're in your early thirties, which of course makes complications more likely, and fertility can decline..."

"But many women have their first babies later these days," Angus interjected.

The consultant nodded. "Yes, they do. And I'm not telling you not to try. You're both healthy, but we've found indication that Amy may have something called endometriosis. Have you heard of this condition?"

Amy shook her head. As the consultant went on to explain that endometriosis was a condition that affects the womb lining and could both decrease her chances of falling pregnant and increase her chances of miscarriage, Amy felt the room begin to spin. On top of the knowledge that she'd lost her precious baby, this was too much to take in. She clutched Angus's hand and only just made it through the rest of the appointment without running from the room.

Standing up as if to dismiss them, and smiling that not-quite smile, the consultant told them to return in a few months for a follow-up visit.

Amy mumbled goodbye and clung to Angus as they trudged out of the consulting room. On the drive home she was silent, staring out the window as the outside world flew past in a blur. She couldn't gather her thoughts.

Angus was silent, too. She desperately wanted to reach out to him and tell him how much she loved him, but that horrible fog seemed to be stopping her. She went into the house and lay on the couch, staring at nothing.

Angus sat next to her, looking lost. Amy watched him, feeling strangely detached from the man she'd loved so much for so long. She mustered a smile as he brought her hand to his mouth and kissed it.

He was a good man. Apart from the blight of not having children early on when they'd begun trying, their marriage had in many ways been perfect. They'd met at college and she'd been instantly attracted to his handsome face, quiet demeanour, and the practical way he got things done without fuss. She'd never expected him to be interested in her, with her loud laugh and inability to stay in one place for two minutes, but the moment their gazes had met they'd both known. When she found out he was a Christian, their fate was set.

He was her rock. She let him gather her into his arms and waited for the tears to come, but even his arms around her couldn't shift the creeping numbness.

"It will be all right, Ames," he whispered into her hair. "I know it will. God will get us through this."

She closed her eyes. She wanted to believe him, she really did, but part of her just couldn't. She felt like nothing would ever be all right ever again. Like this was some kind of cruel joke God was playing on them. It simply wasn't fair.

CHAPTER 1

*A*my stared at the words on the page in front of her. It was the first time she'd been to church since losing the baby, and although she was grateful for the support and all the prayers, she was struggling to connect.

Usually she loved church. She loved the worship, communion and connecting with her friends in faith. For her and Angus, church was the lynchpin of their week, part of the rhythm of their days.

Today, she felt completely out of sync.

Although she'd had many offers to visit over the past two weeks, she'd refused all of them except her parents—they'd come all the way from Adelaide, so she'd had little choice—and of course, Fleur. She felt bad that she was isolating Angus, but when she'd suggested he spend time with friends after work, or go to the gym, he'd refused to leave her alone.

Amy could feel herself slipping. It was as though she were becoming transparent, a ghost in her own world. She'd gone to her Bible for comfort, but instead had found herself turning to passages that described how she felt, like the Psalms...

'The enemy pursues me, he crushes me to the ground, he makes me dwell in the darkness like one long dead. So my spirit grows faint within me, my heart within me is dismayed.'

And the story of Rachel recounted in Matthew, which she'd never paid much attention to before, suddenly came starkly and terribly to life...

'A voice is heard in Ramah, weeping and great mourning, Rachel weeping for her children and refusing to be comforted, because they are no more.'

Although she took comfort from the fact that she could find her feelings mirrored in scripture, she couldn't seem to access the hope and faith that lay on the other side of that. Although she knew in theory that God heard her in her pain, she couldn't seem to connect with that fact. She realised that she'd always taken her faith and belief in God for granted. It had never been tested.

Tuning out the pastor's sermon, she gazed around the church. How many others were coping with the struggles of life right now? With loss and grief and despair? They all looked so happy.

Maybe it wasn't so much her faith in God that was being tested as faith in herself.

After the service ended, she headed straight for the car. Usually she'd stop and chat with everyone, offering to make the tea and arranging events for the coming week. Angus would have to practically drag her home. Now she just wanted to be alone.

As they drove home, she felt Angus looking at her. "How did you find church? Feel any better?" he asked.

"No," she replied, staring out the window.

Angus sighed and she felt suddenly and inexplicably annoyed at him. Why did he not understand she wanted, no, *needed*, to be left alone?

"I picked up a flyer for you about the fashion swap. I know you love things like that," he continued as if she hadn't spoken, "and there are plenty of clothes in your wardrobe you don't wear anymore."

Amy gritted her teeth. Why was he talking to her about clothes? *Was she supposed to care?* "I'm sorry, Angus. I'm not interested in a clothes-swap right now," she replied more tersely than necessary.

He grew quiet. She'd hurt him and instantly felt a pang of guilt. It wasn't okay for her to talk to him like that when he was only trying to cheer her up, but she was tired of everyone trying to cheer her. Why couldn't they just leave her alone?

Some days she even wanted Angus to leave her alone. Then the next she was terrified he would, as if his presence was the only thing holding them together.

"I'm sorry," he said quietly, making her feel even worse.

She should apologise, too, but if she did, it might open a conversation she didn't want to have. Like her, he was hurting as well, and she knew they needed to come together in their grief in order to heal, but part of her didn't want to. She didn't want to heal, because that would mean letting go, and she wasn't ready.

As he pulled the car into their drive, she slid down in her seat. Fleur and Callum were standing at the front door. They hadn't been at church that morning, which was unusual, but Callum was training to be a youth pastor, so Amy guessed they'd been involved with that.

They looked so happy, and there was no missing the fact that this was a newlywed couple deeply in love. It reminded Amy of herself and Angus years ago, before the recent shattering of their dreams. Angus squeezed her hand before they got out of the car and greeted their friends.

Amy looked away and blinked back tears as Fleur embraced her and handed her the bunch of flowers she'd been holding.

"Thank you, they're lovely. Are Will and Lucy not with you?"

"We dropped them at Mum's after Youth Church. Callum gave his first sermon this morning." Pride filled Fleur's face as she glanced at her husband.

"How did it go?" Amy asked, trying to sound interested.

"Good. But how are you?" Rubbing Amy's arm, Fleur studied her with concern-filled eyes.

Amy shrugged. "Not great. Do you want to come inside?"

Fleur nodded and followed her inside the house while Callum and Angus disappeared into the backyard.

Reaching the kitchen, Amy headed for the kettle, but Fleur took over. "Sit down and I'll do it. You look like you need a rest."

Amy sat at the kitchen table and fixed her gaze on her hands.

"How was church?" Fleur asked.

Amy drew a long breath. "I don't know what's wrong with me. I can't seem to connect with anyone."

"Not even God?" Fleur raised a brow.

Amy winced and dropped her shoulders. Sometimes when she was lying awake at night, she felt the whispers of the Spirit, the invitation to come and be comforted, but the grief was too hard and too crystallised. She felt almost as though she was erecting her own cage.

"It's early days, Amy," Fleur said soothingly as she placed a mug of steaming coffee on the table in front of her. "You need time to grieve. And if you want me to pray with you, you only have to ask."

Amy nodded and gave a half-smile. "Thanks." But she felt unworthy. She didn't deserve Fleur. She didn't deserve Angus. This feeling of unworthiness had been creeping up on her over the past few days and was another reason she was resisting opening herself to God, even though she knew deep down He could help her through this if she let Him in.

Fleur sat beside her, hands wrapped around her mug. "How's Angus holding up?"

Amy shrugged. "You know Angus."

"Yes. Callum said he's putting on a brave face." Fleur sighed heavily and put her mug on the table. "Is there anything I can do, Amy? You look so sad. I could stay for a few days if that would help."

Amy shook her head. "I'll be okay."

Fleur gently placed her hand on Amy's wrist. "Amy, sweetheart, I know this is really tough. You need to give yourself time to heal, but try not to push away the people who love you. We're here for you if you'd just let us in."

Amy clenched her mouth tighter. The last thing she wanted to do was push Fleur away, but annoyance bordering on anger seethed inside her, just as it had when Angus tried to comfort her. "I'm not pushing anyone away. I'm just sick of everyone expecting me to get back to normal after what's happened." She couldn't name it, she realised. She couldn't say out loud that she'd lost her baby.

"No one expects that," Fleur said. "I know how hard it is."

"No, no you don't!" Amy snapped before she could stop herself. "You have two beautiful children. You have no idea how I feel, and I wish you would stop pretending you do!"

Fleur sat back in her chair, her eyes as wide as saucers. "I'm not trying to pretend." Pain sounded in her voice. "But even if I haven't had a miscarriage, I know what it's like to suffer loss."

"You have everything you ever wanted," Amy retorted, barely recognising this part of herself and the bitter tone in her voice.

Fleur's expression hardened. "Now, maybe. But have you forgotten that the children and I lost Jeff in battle?"

Amy looked away, instantly ashamed of herself. This wasn't Fleur's fault, and what she'd said to her wasn't fair. She'd been Fleur's support in the years following Jeff's death and she didn't recall her friend having once spoken to her like this. "I'm sorry," she mumbled, and though she meant it, she couldn't bring herself to look at Fleur or say any more. She felt that if she did, she would collapse, that the wall she'd constructed between herself and the outside world was the only thing keeping her from falling apart. From going crazy.

Fleur rubbed her arm. "It's okay, I understand. You'll wade through the pain and climb out the other side eventually, just like I did."

Amy swallowed hard. She could tell by the tone of Fleur's

voice that she was still incredibly hurt, especially when Fleur stood and left her to join the men on the back verandah.

"Are you joining us, Amy?" Angus called through the open door.

"I'm going to lie down," she called back and then went upstairs. All she wanted to do was pull the covers over her head and sink into the mattress and pretend the outside world wasn't there.

But she couldn't sleep. As she thought of how she'd snapped first at Angus and then at Fleur, shame filled her. Fleur was right, she was pushing everybody away and didn't even know how to stop from doing it. She was like Rachel in the Bible, refusing to be comforted, except she couldn't weep. Couldn't even lament for what she'd lost, but could only lie here, feeling the full weight of despair and seemingly unable to reach out to anything or anyone who offered her comfort.

Fleur and Callum shouted goodbye, but she couldn't find the energy to speak.

Angus came in and sat next to her on the bed. She didn't look at him. "What happened with you and Fleur?" he asked gently.

It was obvious, then. Obvious that she was pushing everyone away. She felt desperately tired and flung her hand over her eyes. "I don't know. I just...I'm not in the mood to socialise."

"We're supposed to be at the McCarthy's for a barbecue shortly. It's been booked for weeks but I forgot until Callum reminded me. Shall I phone and cancel?"

When Amy opened her eyes and looked at her husband, she felt a wretchedness of mind she'd never known before. He looked tired and the lines at the corners of his eyes had deepened this past fortnight. "You go," she said softly. "Go and enjoy yourself. It'll do you good."

He hesitated.

"Please," she said, weary again. "I feel a migraine coming on. I need to stay here and have some quiet." She was lying, and she knew he knew she was lying, but neither of them were ready to talk about what was really going on. She was drowning in grief yet resisting any offer of help.

Angus leaned down and kissed her gently on the forehead. "Okay. As long as you're sure. I won't be long."

She didn't look up as he left the room. She listened to him moving around downstairs, and then to him leaving and the car pulling out of their driveway.

She was alone. It was how she preferred to be right now. Being around people was too much effort. She was due to return to work tomorrow and she didn't want to. Not at all. Physically things might be fine, but emotionally and mentally, she was nowhere near ready. She'd recently started a new job as HR manager in Salford's first five-star hotel, and she simply couldn't face everyone.

Without thinking, she pressed a hand to her lower stomach, a habit she hadn't yet managed to shake. The tiny swell that had begun to grow had vanished and her stomach was as soft and flat as before. There was nothing to show, nothing to see. As if there had been no baby.

She wished she could get back to normal, back in the swing of things, but it felt impossible. How could she just forget and return to daily life as if all her dreams hadn't been torn apart and shattered in front of her eyes? Everyone wanted her to, but she would not. She would mourn her child, like Rachel in the land of Ramah.

Except that this creeping exhaustion, this numbness of spirit felt more like deadening than mourning. Unlike Rachel, she could not weep, could not face the pain. She wrapped herself in it but could not look at it.

Because it was your fault, an inner voice whispered, and as soon as she thought it, she felt it was true. Her body was faulty. The endometriosis had probably caused the miscarriage, which meant her body had betrayed her. Her very self was flawed.

If only she'd known...Why had it never occurred to her to get herself checked? Her cycle had always been the bane of her life, but she'd just assumed it was like that for most women.

And now her chances of ever having a healthy child were reduced, and she wasn't getting any younger.

Angus deserves better than you, the voice came again. It was right. They both desperately wanted children, and now Angus was saddled with a wife who might never be able to have them. Even though another part of her tried to soothe her with the knowledge that Angus loved her regardless, that none of this was her fault, the accusing voice boomed louder. She shook her head trying to drown it out, but it only increased.

She had to get away. Perhaps time on her own would help her think clearly and make sense of the situation. If she stayed here, with her guilt and her shame and anger, she would drive everyone away. But where would she go?

Daisy, her cousin, lived on the edge of Melbourne where she ran a homeless shelter. She and Daisy had been close growing up and had stayed in touch via phone and the occasional visit. Daisy was always reminding her she had a spare room if she and Angus ever wanted to come and visit.

With more energy than she'd felt in days, Amy went to the phone and called her. Daisy was glad to hear from her. Clearly Amy's parents had not told the rest of the family the news, perhaps knowing she would need her privacy as much as possible.

"Daisy, I need to ask you something. Can I come and stay for a few days? I need to get away from Salford for a while."

"Of course," her cousin replied, but concern was evident in her voice. "Is everything okay? Are you and Angus all right?"

"Yes, it's not Angus. I just...can I tell you when I get there?" She couldn't bring herself to voice her recent loss.

"You don't have to tell me anything if you don't want to. My door is always open. When do you want to come?"

"Now?"

"Okay..."

Amy ended the call and quickly packed her bag. Now that she had some form of a plan, something to do, she felt energised.

But what about Angus? She couldn't just leave him. She picked up the phone to call, but after staring at the receiver for a few long moments, she replaced it without dialling his number. If she spoke to him, he would try to talk her out of going, and now that she had the chance to get away, the urge to go, to escape, came over her too strongly to ignore.

Instead of calling, she wrote him a short note. It wasn't enough. She was being selfish, but she hoped he would understand. It would be just a few days, and maybe with a change of surroundings she'd come to terms with things. With her loss.

If she stayed here, with the way she was behaving, she could end up losing her husband and her best friend, too.

She bundled her things into her car and set off for Melbourne, a good three-hour drive away, her hands gripping the wheel and her eyes fixed resolutely ahead.

CHAPTER 2

"*A*my's not doing so well," Angus admitted to Callum as they stood at the end of the McCarthy's large back-yard, away from the other guests and just out of earshot. John and Rebecca McCarthy threw a big summer barbecue every year and most people from their church attended, but Angus wished he'd stayed at home. He'd needed to get out of the house, but now that he was here, he just wanted to get home to Amy.

Callum nodded gravely. "Fleur wouldn't tell me what was said, but she seemed really upset. She kept saying that Amy was losing herself, but she also said that these things take time."

"Yes," Angus agreed. "I'm trying to be there for her and give her the time she needs, but it feels like she's freezing me out. I don't know what to do." He sighed heavily, wearily.

Callum gave an understanding nod and lowered his voice.

"And what about you? How are you feeling? I know it must be more acute for Amy, but this is your loss, too, Angus."

Angus sighed. In truth, he didn't know how he was feeling. He was so wrapped up in trying to comfort Amy and look after her that he hadn't had time to sit and process his own feelings. They were there, though. Nagging lumps of pain that brought tears to his eyes when he was alone.

He'd been so excited at the thought of being a father, and Amy would be a great mother. She'd always been naturally nurturing. Now he had to face the idea that they might never get the opportunity to be parents, and it was a blow for which there was no remedy. "I'm just trying to get through a day at a time," he replied honestly.

Callum laid a hand on his arm. Since moving to Salford and meeting and marrying Fleur, he'd become a good friend to Angus. The former Army officer was like him in many ways, a man of few words. They both kept their feelings close to their chest. Callum had seen tremendous loss, serving in wars in East Timor and the Middle East. In comparison, Angus considered himself to have led a charmed life in many ways, although he'd lost his mother to cancer as a young boy. He was close to his father and stepmother, but that sort of loss always left a mark. Angus was surprised how this new wound had touched on the old one, waking up a void in him he didn't know how to fill. He'd been praying hard and, as usual, had received God's comfort, but the fact that Amy would no longer join him in prayer filled him with such sadness.

"We're here for you, mate," Callum said. "Fleur and I are praying for you both."

"Thank you." Angus half turned his head to look at the

garden, afraid tears might fall. "You and Fleur have been amazing."

"Fleur loves Amy, you know that. Whatever went on today, she won't hold a grudge. Amy is bound to not feel herself."

Angus didn't want to say how much the change in Amy was worrying him. His gregarious, outgoing wife seemed to be vanishing before his eyes, locked in a prison whose walls he couldn't breach. In many ways, Amy was the emotional one of the two, while he was the practical one. He got things done, but it was she who breathed life and joy into everything she touched. She was the heart to his hands, and right now he felt a gaping wound, as if he had lost her.

Of course he couldn't tell her that. He had to be the strong one and be there for her. If this was agonising for him, he could only imagine how she must be feeling. What had been a promise and a dream for him had been a tangible reality for her, entwined with her very flesh and blood.

"I don't know how to help her," he said. "I'm trying, but most of the time I sense she'd rather I wasn't there. I know it's early days and she needs time, but I'm watching her sink and I can't do anything about it..." He stopped as a wave of grief threatened to consume him.

"I hear you," Callum said. "You're like me. You want to do something. Fix it. I guess sometimes we have to step back and let nature take its course and accept that we can't control everything. God's got this, Angus. It might not feel like it now, but He'll lead you through this valley and you'll both come out the other side."

"I know," Angus said, sounding more resolute than he felt. But he did know. God was both comforter and sustainer, and more than they could ever conceptualise. He had to trust that everything would ultimately turn out for the best. His mother would have told him that. Through her long illness, her faith had never wavered once, and it was an example Angus had carried with him his entire life.

"I should get back to Amy," he said, checking his watch. The time had slipped by and it was early evening. He hoped she'd been able to get some sleep. He followed Callum to the crowd of people standing on the decking to say his goodbyes.

Fleur kissed him on the cheek and squeezed his hand, concern filling her eyes. "Tell Amy I'll phone her tomorrow. And not to worry about today."

Again, Angus wondered what had been said, but decided not to ask. It was between the two of them, after all. Amy and Fleur's friendship had always been unbreakable and he was sure that wasn't about to change now.

Angus drove home and let himself in. The house was quiet and dark. He hoped Amy was still asleep and not lying lost in her own thoughts as she was so prone to do lately. He went upstairs to check on her and opened the bedroom door quietly.

She wasn't there.

A chill ran through him, but he tried to assure himself he was being silly, even as he checked the bathroom and then all but sprinted down the stairs to look in the front room and the kitchen. Surely, he would find her sitting in the shadows some-where. There was no need for the sudden anxiety that gnawed at his gut.

Except she wasn't downstairs either. After checking the yard, he ran out onto the drive and opened the garage door.

Her car was gone.

Trying to swallow his panic, he rushed back into the house, turning all the lights on. Then he saw the note on the dining room table and breathed a sigh of relief. She'd probably just gone to get some groceries. Or perhaps some supplies for work. That was good, if she was getting up and out again, that was good.

But when he read the note, his stomach sank.

Dear Angus,

I'm so sorry to do this to you and with no notice, but I feel like I'm going crazy here. I know I'm pushing you and Fleur and everyone away and I want you to know I'm sorry. You have been nothing but supportive and I couldn't ask for a better husband.

Angus took a deep breath and mentally steeled himself before he continued reading. He had a terrible thought... was she leaving him?

I love you so much, Angus, and I don't want you to think this is about me and you in any way. I need some time alone to get my head and my emotions straight before I make everything worse. Please don't think I'm abandoning you. I'm not. I remain forever yours.

Angus let out his breath in a deep sigh of relief.

I've gone to stay with my cousin Daisy in Melbourne for a few days. I need to be away for a time. I'll phone you in a few days and will be thinking of you in the meantime. I understand if you're angry with me, but I love you and I hope to use this time to get back on my feet. I hope you can understand.

Always yours,

Amy

Putting the note down, he rested his head in his hands, a heavy invisible weight crushing his shoulders. He did understand, of course he did. It had occurred to him a few days before to suggest that she take some time away to stay with Daisy or her parents, but he hadn't wanted to say it in case she took offence. So yes, he understood. But for her to take off like this, without a proper goodbye, without even consulting him? It wasn't like her. It wasn't like *them*. He'd always prided himself on their egalitarian marriage. They were a team, they made decisions together. They didn't run off when things got tough.

But then, things had never been this tough before. And now he truly felt like he was losing her as well as their baby.

He clasped his hands together and closed his eyes. "Lord God, I feel so overwhelmed. My heart is distressed. Be with Amy, Lord. Comfort her. Help her. I don't know what else to do apart from pray."

Too upset for more words, he continued to pour out his grief silently. Slowly, the comforting presence of the Holy Spirit surrounded him. Filled him. He was hurting, and hurting badly, but God would carry him through. Even so, a thought lingered in the back of his mind and haunted him as he went to bed alone.

What if she never came back?

CHAPTER 3

*A*my woke the next morning, disoriented as she struggled to remember where she was. The sheets felt rougher than usual and the light from the window shone in at an unfamiliar angle.

Then she remembered. She sat and glanced around the sparsely furnished room. She'd left home. Not forever, but even so, it had been a sudden and unplanned move and was so unlike her she didn't know how she felt.

There was relief. Relief at being away from the pressure of going back to work and having to face the sympathetic smiles and concerned questions which, however well-meaning, felt intrusive and hollow. She'd need to call in sick, but she'd do that a little later. Relief that she could simply focus on herself and not worry about the effect she was having on Angus. Or Fleur. Relief that she didn't have to sit in church and feel that she was suddenly an outsider. That where once she'd been at home, she suddenly felt in some kind of emotional exile, as if her soul was a desert she didn't know how to cross.

There was guilt, too. Sharp and painful. She thought of Angus and felt an ache in her heart. After weeks of feeling more and more estranged, she'd wanted his comforting arms around her and his promises that as long as they were together, everything would be okay.

Except they hadn't been. It hadn't been okay at all.

Pushing her thoughts away, Amy swung out of bed and pulled on her dressing gown. Her movements felt heavy and wooden, a familiar feeling these days. Her grief weighed her down like a cloak she couldn't shake off. Although being at Daisy's would mean that some of the pressure was off, she doubted anything could truly take this weight from her. Not even God. It was as though she was wading through quicksand.

She went downstairs to find Daisy sitting at the breakfast bar, reading the morning paper.

She looked up and smiled as Amy came in. "Good morning." She pushed a plate of croissants and jam towards her. "There's fresh coffee in the pot. Would you like some?"

Amy nodded and managed a smile. The croissant looked delicious, but she had no appetite and she nibbled it unenthusiastically. If Daisy noticed, she didn't say anything.

"Angus called," Daisy told her. "He said not to wake you, he just wanted to make sure you'd gotten here safely and are okay. He said he'd phone your employer and square a few days off."

"I can do that," Amy said, then realised she sounded ungrateful.

Daisy shrugged. "I'm just relaying the message."

Amy felt bad. She should be grateful that everyone was being so kind, yet somehow, she just felt stifled. "Did he sound...all right?" she asked, feeling guilty again. She'd done the right thing by getting away, but she shouldn't have left without speaking to him. He deserved better. Why couldn't she bring herself to face him? Or even call him?

"He sounded concerned," Daisy said honestly, closing the paper and looking at her cousin with shrewdness in her grey eyes. "Have you come here to get some space, Amy, or have you come here to hide?"

Amy blinked, startled and immediately defensive. "If you don't want me to stay..." she began, but Daisy held up a hand to silence her.

"Don't do that. You know you're welcome, and for as long as you want. But I'm not going to mollycoddle you, my sweet, any more than I did when we were children."

Amy couldn't help but smile at that. Daisy was a few years older than her and as children had seemed the only one in their family impervious to Amy's charms. Amy had used her golden curls and big blue eyes to great effect when it came to getting her own way. Daisy had never fallen for it for a minute.

"What are you going to do today?" Daisy asked.

Amy shrugged. She hadn't planned on doing anything.

"If you simply want to rest, that's fine. I'll be at the shelter most of the day, so if you want to come down at any time, we could always use an extra pair of hands."

Amy didn't answer. As awful as it would sound, the last thing she felt like doing was helping out at Daisy's shelter. She admired her cousin for the tireless work she put into helping others, but right now, Amy didn't feel she had anything to give.

She felt a pervading sense of uselessness that had been present ever since she'd learned about the endometriosis. It had sapped every ounce of creativity out of her. She hadn't baked once. Even ladling soup at Daisy's shelter felt beyond her. "Maybe tomorrow," she said.

Daisy gave her a sharp look but nodded. "Fair enough. Make yourself at home. There's cable TV and I've still got that bookshelf full of Nana's books. Honestly, she was into all sorts —culture, travel, you name it, it's there. You should be able to entertain yourself."

Amy nodded. All she really wanted to do was go back to bed, but it felt wrong to say that to Daisy when she was about to spend her entire day in service to others.

Daisy bustled off to get ready for the day ahead and Amy went back upstairs. She laid some clothes out, sweatpants and a shirt, wishing she'd packed her old comfy vest, and reluc-tantly took a shower. She felt so fragile that the water pattering her skin was almost painful.

She studiously avoided looking at her naked body. The body that had let her down. Since the miscarriage, she'd not wanted to look at herself, to see the way the swollenness of her breasts and the tiny swell of her lower stomach had so quickly disappeared, as if they had never been there at all.

As if her baby had never been.

She stepped out of the shower and got dressed, her limbs wooden and heavy again. Just the interaction with Daisy over breakfast had been more than she had been managing most mornings and she was exhausted already. At the same time, she felt a tiny bit of the old Amy rear her head and she decided she could at least go downstairs.

Once Daisy left, she spent the morning looking through the bookshelf containing their grandmother's old books. Nana had been an interesting woman and her reading tastes reflected her many interests. Amy found herself lost for a few hours reading about the English Land Girls in World War Two before her stomach grumbled, reminding her that it was lunch time. It was the first time in days she'd felt physically hungry. She fixed a salad and then had a slice of the sponge cake Daisy had left out for her. Feeling a little brighter, she turned the TV on and settled down to watch some daytime shows.

When a program about early motherhood came on, taking her unawares, Amy felt like she'd been punched in the gut. She stared at the screen, watching a new mother place her baby in its crib. Tears stung her eyes. She turned the TV off and went upstairs, retreating under her bed covers. Daisy had been right —she was hiding.

Later that evening she joined Daisy downstairs, although she declined an evening meal, her appetite having fled once more. Daisy poured a cup of tea and chattered about her day. Despite herself, Amy felt more than a little interested.

The shelter Daisy ran was always overcrowded and under-funded, and it sounded as though it sometimes kept going on prayer alone. They housed homeless and vulnerable people and had both short-term beds, known as 'rough sleepers', and a handful of individual rooms that were usually reserved for younger women or the particularly vulnerable.

"This girl, Marta, has been with us for a few weeks now. She's only seventeen so I'm hoping Social Services will get her properly housed soon, but she's not overly forthcoming about her circumstances. I gather she ran away from foster care about a year ago and has been living with her boyfriend since then. Now she's run away from him."

Amy shuddered. "Was he violent?"

Daisy's jaw tightened. "We think so. She doesn't say a lot, but she's obviously terrified of him. He'd been plying her with drugs, too."

Amy shook her head. How could people do that?

"The good news," Daisy went on, "is that Marta has been coming to church. We're a Christian shelter but we don't push faith on anyone. Marta asked to come of her own accord and recently made a commitment."

Amy smiled. Marta's story had momentarily taken her outside of herself. "I'm glad for her," she said, meaning it. There were too many lost souls in the world. She was glad the girl had started to find her way home, although it sounded as though her journey hadn't been, and wouldn't be, an easy one.

Daisy looked at Amy, her brow furrowed. "Why don't you come and meet her tomorrow? It would do you good to get out of your own head and I'm sure she'd like the company. We're always so short staffed at the shelter that I never get to spend as much time with individuals as I'd like. Maybe you could come and sit with her a while?"

Amy frowned. "What would I say? I wouldn't want her to think I was being intrusive. She's obviously been through a lot."

"She likes to cook, although her skills are limited. Perhaps you could teach her some basics."

Amy shifted uncomfortably. She knew Daisy meant well, but she'd come here for a break, not to take on a girl with problems when she couldn't even face her own.

Daisy saw her reluctance and smiled, although Amy could sense her disappointment. "Don't worry. I understand if it's too much. I just thought it could be an option if you get fed up hanging around here."

Amy nodded. "Sure. I'll see how I feel tomorrow."

Later, as she lay in bed, she thought about the young girl and how lonely she must be feeling tonight. Then her thoughts turned to Angus and she wondered how he was getting on without her. Fleur and Callum would have rallied around him, no doubt. Although it was hypocritical of her, she'd asked him for time on her own, but she was disappointed he hadn't phoned her today. Didn't he miss her?

Closing her eyes, she prayed for him. It was the first time she'd prayed in a while and it was a comfort, although she couldn't bring herself to pray about the things that were really on her heart. Instead, she prayed for Marta, a young girl she didn't know but whose story, for some reason, had touched her heart.

Before she drifted off to sleep, she decided she'd go to the shelter tomorrow after all.

CHAPTER 4

"*A*my, this is Marta," Daisy said the following day when Amy arrived at the shelter mid-morning.

The girl looked warily at Amy. Marta was thin, with brown hair pulled back in a clip, dressed in baggy clothes, and her arms crossed protectively across herself as if she wanted to hide away from the world. Amy knew how she felt.

"Hi, I'm Amy, Daisy's cousin." Amy offered a warm smile.

"Amy's staying with me for a while," Daisy added.

Marta looked interested and gave Amy a curious look.

"I wonder if you could give Amy something to do in the kitchen today?" Daisy asked.

"You can chop," the girl said.

Amy smiled and nodded, then threw a look at Daisy, who grinned and then left her with Marta. Glancing around the kitchen, Amy knew she would have to stop herself from taking over. As a hobby, she'd done some catering over the years and it had been a long time since she'd been relegated to chopping duty, but not wanting to appear proud, she washed her hands, threw on an apron and let Marta direct her.

"How are you finding it here?' she asked, as she started chopping what looked like a never-ending pile of carrots. The soup kitchen was open for all the homeless in the area, not just those staying at the shelter, so Daisy informed her they needed to make a lot of soup. It was going to be a long day.

"It's good. I'm safe here," Marta replied shortly.

Amy studied the girl, shocked by her matter of fact tone. Being safe was something Amy had always taken for granted. Of course, she knew that wasn't everyone's experience, but to hear the girl speak so bluntly brought it home. She could only imagine what it must be like to feel unsafe on a daily basis.

"Are you a Christian?" Marta asked out of the blue, surprising her.

Amy nodded. "Yes, I am. Are you?"

Marta's pale face lit up as she answered. "Yes. Just these past few weeks since I've been here. I'd heard about God, but I'd never taken much notice. I went to church with Daisy the first Sunday I was here to see what it was about, and I had this feeling that there was someone out there who truly loved me. Afterwards, Daisy led me to God." Marta returned her attention to the potatoes.

Amy stared at her for a moment, envying the girl her new and simple faith. She'd obviously been through so much, more than Amy could ever fathom, yet she'd found God in the midst of it all. Whereas Amy, brought up in faith, was floundering.

"I'm so glad you've found Him," Amy said softly. "It can't be easy, staying here."

There was a trace of laughter in Marta's voice. "I've been in worse places, trust me. This is nice. People care, and that's what's important. Most people don't." She sliced a potato with a sudden viciousness that gave Amy an insight into her inner feelings.

"I'm sorry for whatever you've been through," Amy said, feeling awkward because she didn't really know what to say.

Marta gave her a look as though sizing her up, and then seemed to decide she could trust her. "I was in care. My mum died when I was twelve. She was an alcoholic, but she still loved me, and I miss her."

Amy did her best to hide a grimace. She wondered where Marta's father was but decided not to ask.

"I was going to college. I wanted to study law," Marta continued, surprising Amy, "but then I met Steve. I thought he loved me. I really did." The girl went quiet and turned away, concentrating on the potatoes once again.

Amy felt the wave of pain that radiated from her and felt a sudden urge to embrace her, though she doubted Marta would welcome it. Whoever Steve was, he had clearly hurt her badly. Amy carried on chopping carrots, a little more vigorously now. The little Marta had told her had wakened her out of her stupor. She felt angry at the obvious injustice the girl had suffered and at the man who had hurt her. The world could be a cruel place, she reflected.

Once the soup was simmering, Marta removed her apron and left the kitchen, leaving Amy with a shy but genuine smile.

Despite herself, Amy felt pleased. Although she hadn't said much, she felt that she'd made a connection with Marta. If nothing else, she'd been able to focus on someone other than herself and her own pain for a while.

Daisy came in to check on her, a sheen of sweat on her cheeks.

"Everything all right?" Amy asked.

"Yes, we've just had a new admission and it's a bit hectic, that's all. Finish up if you like. The volunteers will be coming to dish up soon."

Nodding, Amy removed her apron, surprised that she felt disappointed. She walked the few blocks back to Daisy's, feeling more alive than she had in a long time. She was surprised at how much she'd enjoyed chopping carrots and preparing the soup. It had been nice to simply do some basic tasks.

Reaching Daisy's house, she went inside, and instead of heading for the couch, she strolled through to the kitchen. A tin of ham and half a carton of eggs sat on the counter. Amy presumed Daisy had them out for dinner. She inspected the fridge and then the cupboards and decided to rustle up a ham and egg pie. By the time Daisy walked in, the pie was browning in the oven and a pasta dish was chilled and stored ready for their lunch the following day.

Daisy's eyes widened as Amy took the pie out of the oven. "Wow, Amy. That smells great. Thank you!"

Amy grinned. "You're welcome. I've made lunch for tomorrow, too." She leaned against the counter and folded her arms. "I was wondering if I could come to the shelter again tomorrow. I enjoyed being there today, as well as talking to Marta."

Daisy smiled. "I'm glad you two got on. She doesn't talk much normally."

Amy thought of the things Marta had told her, about her mother and the boyfriend she hadn't elaborated on, but who had clearly been the source of much pain. She then thought of how lucky she was to have Angus and realised that she missed him very much. She'd phone him soon. Maybe even tonight. But then she wondered...was she really ready?

CHAPTER 5

$\mathcal{T}$aking his seat at the Bible study group at the McCarthy's, Angus offered everyone a smile while trying to hide his sadness at being there without Amy. They usually came together, every fortnight like clockwork.

"Is Amy ill?" Rebecca asked, giving him a sympathetic smile.

He went to say yes, and then decided it was best to be honest. "She's gone to stay with her cousin in Melbourne for a few days. A bit of a break for her." Not too honest, of course. He wasn't about to tell the study group that Amy had just upped and left without telling him, that he hadn't spoken to her in two days, and that he had no idea when she was coming home. He didn't want to be here tonight, but anything had to better than spending his third night watching reruns of golf tournaments and trying not to worry about Amy and their future.

A woman he didn't recognise looked at him curiously from across the room. About his age, she was slim and attractive with long dark hair. She approached with a smile and extended her hand. "Hello, I'm Cherie. I moved into the area last month. I think I've seen you at church a few times."

Angus shook her hand, trying to muster up some social skills. He wasn't in the mood for chit-chat but vaguely remembered being introduced to her at church a few weeks ago. If he remembered correctly, she was not long widowed. "Nice to see you again," he said politely.

She held his gaze and he noticed how green her eyes were before he looked away, sat down and took out his Bible.

They were working their way through the Psalms, one of his favourite books in the Bible. It was fitting, because of how he felt at the moment. He loved the way the Psalms ran the gamut of human emotions and back again, yet always ended up praising God. He'd always found them a comfort in difficult times, and this was certainly one of those times.

They were up to Psalm twenty-seven. Cherie offered to read it out, and Angus found himself transfixed by her melodious voice.

The Lord is my light and my salvation—whom shall I fear? The Lord is the stronghold of my life—of whom shall I be afraid? When the wicked advance against me to devour me, it is my enemies and my foes that will stumble and fall. Though an army besiege me, my heart will not fear; though war break out against me, even then I will be confident.

One thing I ask from the Lord, this only do I seek: that I may dwell in the house of the Lord all the days of my life, to gaze on the beauty of the Lord and to seek Him in His temple. For in the day of trouble He will keep me safe in His dwelling; He will hide me in the shelter of His sacred tent and set me high upon a rock. Then my head will be exalted above the enemies who surround me; at His sacred tent I will sacrifice with shouts of joy; I will sing and make music to the Lord.

Hear my voice when I call, Lord; be merciful to me and answer me. My heart says of you "Seek His face!" Your face, Lord, I will seek. Do not hide Your face from me, do not turn Your servant away in anger; You have been my helper. Do not reject me or forsake me, God my Saviour. Though my father and mother forsake me, the Lord will receive me. Teach me Your way, Lord; lead me in a straight path because of my oppressors. Do not turn me over to the desire of my foes, for false witnesses rise up against me, spouting malicious accusations. I remain confident of this: I will see the goodness of the Lord in the land of the living. Wait for the Lord; be strong and take heart and wait for the Lord.'

Tears pricked the corners of his eyes as he breathed in the beautiful words of hope and praise. *It will be all right. I just have to trust.*

He looked up to see Cherie watching him. He wiped his eyes quickly, not wanting to show his distress to the group. "That was beautifully read," he said quietly.

She smiled shyly.

"It was indeed," John McCarthy said. "This passage really speaks to me of how God always receives us with grace and never turns His face away, no matter what's going on in our lives. We only have to seek Him. But we do have to *seek* Him."

"This Psalm was a great comfort to me after I lost my husband," Cherie said to the group. "It's so tempting to listen to the voices of despair and anger, but God is always there, inviting us to dwell with Him. We have to make God our rock and our refuge, otherwise we stumble."

Angus felt humbled by this woman's obvious faith in the face of such tremendous loss. He hoped someone had introduced her to Fleur, who would be the ideal mentor for her. Thinking of Amy and their own loss, he looked down at his Bible while he addressed the group. "Be strong and take heart and wait for the Lord." He swallowed hard and glanced at the circle of friends. "This verse really speaks to me right now. You all know about my and Amy's loss. It's hit her—us—so hard." He swallowed again. "I feel like all we can do in this season is stay strong and wait on the Lord for a breakthrough. This scripture gives me hope."

There were murmurs of comfort as Angus finished. They discussed the text for a while then held hands and prayed for each other and all those in the church who needed support. When Rebecca prayed for Amy, although a wave of sadness swept over him, he had the sense of being held by both the love and care of his friends and God Himself. He was glad he'd come.

They dispersed into the kitchen for hot drinks and cake. Angus was pouring himself a cup of tea when Cherie approached him, her face creased with concern. She laid a hand on his arm. "I'm sorry to hear about your wife," she said softly.

Angus smiled, although he found himself stepping back a little. She was a lovely woman, but she seemed a little forward. Then he felt guilty—she was just being friendly. "Thank you," he said sincerely. "It's been tough. I'm sure the break will do her good." He was mortified to hear his breath catch.

Cherie looked at him with narrowed eyes. "Did you not want her to go?"

Sighing, he gave a reluctant shrug. It was a relief to admit what was really going on, and Cherie's large green eyes held nothing but kindness. She understood what it was like to feel loss better than he did, after all. "She left a note. I didn't know."

Cherie's eyes enlarged further. "Oh, but that's awful! You poor thing. She must be terribly upset to abandon you like that."

Angus suddenly felt bad and wished he hadn't said anything. It was his and Amy's business as man and wife, no one else's. Especially not this stranger's. But as much as he truly did understand Amy's actions, he also did feel abandoned by her. That was the right word for how he was feeling, even if it wasn't quite the reality. Shrugging again, he drained his cup and smiled absent-mindedly at Cherie. "I think I'll head home now." He quickly said his goodbyes to everyone and drove home. He needed to speak to his wife.

Once inside, he took his phone from his pocket and dialled her number. For a long moment he thought she wasn't going to answer. Finally, she did. His heart ached at the flatness in her voice.

"How are you?" he asked cautiously.

"I'm not sure yet. What about you? How are you doing?"

He took a deep breath. He needed to be honest with her. Tiptoeing around their feelings had resulted in this situation in the first place. "I'm glad to hear your voice. I've missed you a lot these past few days, Amy. The house is empty without you."

When she didn't answer, his heart shrivelled a little further. He would do anything for just one warm gesture from her, one kind word. Did she really not understand that he was hurting, too?

He squeezed his eyes shut and pinched the bridge of his nose. "I understand why you went to Daisy's." He did his best to keep his voice steady. As awful as he felt, it wasn't right to burden her with his feelings, even if they were weighing so heavily on him that he was starting to wonder when he might break. "But I'm upset you didn't tell me before you left."

"I'm sorry." Although her voice was small, there was a hint of emotion instead of that awful flatness.

He massaged the back of his neck. "It's okay. Do you know when you might be coming home?" He winced at the neediness in his own voice. He should be stronger than this. He had to be stronger than this.

Another silence. He could hear her breathing, and the urge to put his arms around her was overwhelming.

"I...I need time, Angus."

He swallowed his disappointment. "Okay. Whatever you need. How much time can you take off work?"

"I've got plenty of holiday leave. At least another three weeks."

That would mean their summer holiday plans would be dashed. Although right now, the idea of going away on holiday and enjoying each other's company again felt a million years away. The sudden distance between them was vast, much wider than the miles to Melbourne.

She may as well be on the other side of the world.

"I might not stay that long," she added, and he felt a flicker of hope. "It's just...I can't cope with seeing everyone right now. The pity in their faces..."

The note of bitterness in her tone shocked him. It was so unlike the Amy he knew and loved. But anything was better than the numbness. Perhaps she was finally starting to process what had happened. If she had to go to Melbourne to do that, then he mustn't stand in her way. He had to give her what she needed—he only wished it was easier to handle. He'd always assumed that if anything bad happened they'd stick together and see each other through. Wasn't that what being married was about? He realised that he too was carrying resentment and immediately felt guilty. They needed to talk and needed badly to connect, but how could they if she didn't want to see him?

"Everyone cares about you. It's not just pity, Amy. It's love." He thought it best, given her present mood, not to tell her they'd prayed for her as a group at Bible study.

"It feels like pity."

"Well, I love you," he said softly, all but willing the strength of his love to travel the wires and reach her. Penetrate the layers she had wrapped around herself.

"I love you, too," she said back, but the words lacked emotion.

He thought back to the note she'd left. She was grieving, and so lost in that grief she couldn't see outside of it. He had to give her time and keep praying for her, trusting that the Lord would bring her through. He thought of the words of the Psalm the group had read earlier. *'Be strong, take heart and wait for the Lord.'* That was all he could do.

"I'm here for you, Amy," he said, his voice stronger now. Stronger than he felt, anyway. "Take as long as you need, but make sure you call me. Let me know how you are. Whenever you're ready, I can take some time off, too, and come and see you, or we could go away together."

There was silence again and he knew he'd pushed too far, too quick. He had to accept that she needed time alone. They had the rest of their lives together—surely he could give her a few days or even a few weeks if that was what she required.

If only it didn't feel like she was inexorably slipping away from him. "Don't worry," he said before she could answer. "I'll wait for you to let me know what you need."

"Thank you," she said.

He wasn't sure if it was wishful thinking, but she sounded a touch warmer. "So, how's Daisy?" he asked, changing the topic.

When she answered, the sudden, brighter note in her voice surprised him. "She's good. You know she runs the homeless shelter? I went with her yesterday and helped out for a while in the kitchen."

Angus felt a spark of hope. He'd strongly suspected Amy would be in bed all day at Daisy's like she'd been at home, and had been worried that the trip would only deepen her depression. Instead, she was spending time helping others.

Yet, along with the hope and the pride in her for not giving up, he also felt another flare of resentment. Why could she, his wife, rouse herself to serve food to strangers but could barely speak to her own husband? It felt unfair. He took a deep breath and prayed for calm to embrace him, reminding himself to be patient. To stay strong and take heart.

"That's great," he said, trying to sound happy for her. He *was* happy, he told himself firmly.

"Yes, I was surprised by how much I enjoyed it. I'm going back tomorrow."

"That's great," he said again, deliberately forcing enthusiasm.

43

"Okay. Well, I'd better go. I'm tired," she said and suddenly she did sound weary again, as if the simple act of talking to him had exhausted her.

"Goodnight," he said softly.

"Goodnight."

"I love you," he added, but she'd already gone and he was talking to thin air. Sighing, he slipped the phone back into his pocket, feeling that void again. He trudged upstairs and went into their bedroom. The house was empty without her, the bed an expanse of loneliness without her next to him. He sat down and put his head in his hands.

The word Cherie had used came to mind again, the word that precisely captured how he felt. *Abandoned.* No matter how much he tried to tell himself that he was overreacting and would soon have his wife home, he was drowning in emotions that conflicted and tussled with one another. He was trying to be strong for Amy, just like the Psalm said, but he also felt as though his own heart was in tatters, and who did he have to turn to? He'd been devastated at losing the baby, too, but he couldn't give voice to that, couldn't ask for empathy. Not in the face of Amy's greater pain.

He rubbed his hand over his eyes, suddenly exhausted himself. There was no escape. No opportunity for him to simply drive off into the night and stay with a family member. To not go to work and desert everybody. He shook his head sharply as if the movement would clear his mind of such thoughts. He brought the Psalm to mind again as he closed his eyes.

Let me seek Your face, Lord, even in the face of distress. Dwell with me in my darkest moments, dear Lord, and be with Amy, too. Strengthen and comfort us both.

Feeling somewhat calmer, he undressed, showered, and climbed into bed. He tried to keep his mind on the comforting words and as he did, he recalled the beauty of Cherie's voice reading them out. He wished Amy had been there to hear it.

He rolled over, realising once again how large and empty the bed was without her beside him, and fell into a restless sleep.

CHAPTER 6

"*A*re you coming to the prayer meeting tonight?" Marta asked as she looked up at Amy hopefully.

Amy felt her heart lift a little at the girl's eagerness. Being around her was doing her good. She'd started to call Angus again last night but had put the phone down before it rang. She didn't know what was wrong with her. Although her exile was self-imposed, she missed him, but at the same time, it was as though there was this impenetrable fog between them. She couldn't talk to him or even picture his face without feeling the pain of her loss stab through her. Angus and her love for him were so tied up with the pain of losing the baby that it was much easier to simply push it all away.

But she was hurting him. She'd heard it in his voice when they'd spoken. As much as he'd tried to be understanding, she'd heard the anguish in his voice, the disbelief that she'd upped and left. A part of her felt rebellious. Why couldn't she leave if she wanted to? Why, for once in her life, could she not be jolly, bubbly Amy?

She immediately felt guilty and turned her attention back to Marta, thinking how the girl was positively glowing with health today. She'd braided her hair and there was some colour in her cheeks. She was prettier than Amy first realised.

Amy smiled at her. "Yes, that would be lovely. Daisy did mention it this morning."

They were sitting in the recreation room having a break after the busy lunch period. Amy had been impressed at how tirelessly the girl worked and how she had a kind word for everyone who came in. Considering what Marta had obviously been through, that openness was refreshing.

It even made Amy feel a little inferior. How could she give up at the first hurdle of her life when this young woman had obviously had nothing but hurdles her entire life, and yet here she was, excited about the prayer meeting? "Your faith is inspiring," Amy told her truthfully.

Marta smiled shyly. "It's saved me," she said quietly. "It really has. I never thought someone like me would be welcome in a church."

"Someone like you?" Amy frowned and leaned forward. "Marta, nothing that happened in your life was your fault. Not that your mother...that you ended up in care." She stopped, unsure what to say.

Marta's face twisted. Her voice was hollow when she spoke, her youthful eagerness gone. "Maybe not when I was young, but I got into some bad stuff when I was with Steve. Drugs. Look." She rolled up her sleeve. Small red marks dotted the crook of her arm near her veins.

Amy bit her lip to keep from gasping. She didn't want Marta to feel judged. She wasn't judging her, but she did feel a wave of righteous anger at Steve, who had clearly exploited this brave young woman. "That's not your fault either," she said firmly. "If you don't mind me saying so, this Steve seems like a predator. You're incredibly brave to have gotten away. So many young women don't."

Marta ducked her head, clearly embarrassed at the praise. "I guess I can see that now. He's nearly ten years older than me. If I didn't do what he wanted, he hit me. It was easier to take the drugs, then I could block out what was happening."

Amy felt as if her heart would break. She reached over and took Marta's hand. Marta didn't pull away, although she wouldn't meet Amy's gaze.

"You're safe here, Marta. I can hardly imagine what you've been through, but I know this much—you have nothing to be ashamed of. That man should have known better. God sees that. He sees *you*, not just the things you've done or the things that have happened to you." Amy felt something stir inside as she spoke and wondered if her last sentence wasn't directed as much at herself as it was at Marta.

Marta smiled again and nodded. "I know, I do feel that God sees *me*, my heart. Daisy told me the story of the woman who threw herself at Jesus' feet. The one where she's crying and everyone else is saying she's a sinner and He shouldn't talk to her. But He ignored them. He told her that she was forgiven. Like you said, he saw *her*, not whatever had happened that caused the men to say those things about her. When I saw it written right there in the Bible, it changed things for me completely."

Marta fell silent. She looked down, as if embarrassed about sharing so much.

Amy squeezed her hand again. "I think you're amazing," she said softly.

Marta looked up and grinned. "Thanks. But what about you? Why are *you* here?"

Amy wanted to tell her about losing the baby and leaving Angus, but found she didn't have the words. It was as though there was still a wall around her feelings that she didn't dare climb. "I just needed some time alone. My husband and I, we weren't getting on." She felt herself colour, not knowing if that was a half-truth or a half-lie.

Then she felt guilty when Marta nodded her head knowingly. "Was he bad to you, too?"

"No! No, Angus is...well everything you could ask for, really. It's me. I don't know what's going on with me." A wave of sadness swept through her that she couldn't hold back.

"Maybe the prayer meeting will help," Marta said.

Amy nodded gratefully. "Yes, maybe it will."

LATER, they sat in the small sanctuary room that served as a chapel, a one-to-one room, and an emergency sleeping space in the winter when the shelter was over capacity. In attendance were Amy, Daisy and Marta, a few of the volunteers, and two other residents from the shelter. They sat in a circle and Daisy handed a Bible to each.

"We've been praying through the Psalms," Marta whispered to Amy, who felt a jolt go through her. Her Bible study group at home had been looking at the Psalms, too. She'd enjoyed studying them with Angus.

They read Psalm twenty-seven mindfully, taking a line each and pausing in between to let the words sink in. Despite herself, Amy felt the wall she'd constructed inside her start to crumble. So terrified of feeling anything, she realised she'd even done her best to block out God and His comforting presence she knew could sustain and nourish her if only she would allow Him in. He was her rock and her refuge, and she'd been blocking Him out as well as Angus and her friends.

She bowed her head and let the words wash over her.

"For in the day of trouble He will keep me safe in His dwelling; He will hide me in the shelter of His sacred tent and set me high upon a rock," Marta read.

Tears pricked the corner of Amy's eyes. She'd been retreating into herself, seeking her own shelter instead of trusting in God, which had only resulted in locking herself away in her own prison and then running into self-imposed exile. While the thought of going home still filled her with panic, she felt something open inside her. A tiny crack to let the light in.

When it reached her turn to read, she hesitated and had to take a deep breath before she could voice the words of Scripture. She hadn't read aloud from the Word since before...everything.

"Hear my voice when I call, Lord; be merciful to me and answer me. My heart says of You seek His face! Your face, Lord, I will seek. Do not hide Your face from me, do not turn Your servant away in anger; You have been my helper."

Her voice caught in her throat as she read, and she had to

blink tears away. She could feel Marta's and Daisy's eyes on her, and even though she knew they were only looking at her with love, she felt raw and vulnerable.

As they reflected on the verse, she realised it spoke to her deeply. Her heart was calling to her to seek His face. The problem was unlike that of the writer of the Psalm, because she was the one turning away in anger. Turning away from the mercy and help she knew was waiting for her if she would only seek it.

When the Psalm had been read, they sat in quiet contemplation and prayer for some time before Marta spoke. Amy listened with admiration. An inner strength and assurance shone through the girl when she spoke about the Word and its meaning to her.

"This reminds me of how I felt when I first came here," she said, an openness in her voice that made Amy's heart ache. "I was so lost, so angry and broken, but I was crying out for help, too. Seeking something to fill the void I carried. It was when I cried out, like, deep in my soul, that God answered me and I knew finally that He was real. That He'd always been there, even when, like the Psalm said, I was faced with oppression and enemies and people who wanted to do me harm." She paused and her face twisted the way it had earlier when she'd spoken of Steve.

Amy smiled at her encouragingly. The girl's story was a harrowing one, but ultimately triumphant, just like the Psalm.

"What I love," Marta continued, her expression calm again, "is that the Bible isn't just all holy and spiritual and choirs of angels and stuff. It's real. It speaks about real things that go on in life. Even King David had to cry out for help, and he felt persecuted and under attack. But he cried out to God and God answered him. That's all we have to do. Like Jesus said, seek and you will find." She fell silent, looking a little embarrassed as she bent her head over her Bible again, avoiding the nods and smiles of the group.

Amy stared at her and felt incredibly humble. Marta's faith and her journey, though still clearly new and ongoing, were so inspiring. And she was right. Life did get real. Nowhere did Scripture say that leading a life of faith would be easy or shield one from sorrows and challenges. For the first time she admitted to herself that she'd been angry with God for the loss of her baby. Even worse was the fact that she'd begun to believe the lie that it was some kind of punishment. She hadn't lost her baby because she'd done anything wrong, but because loss was a part of life. She didn't have to understand it. She just had to listen to the call of her heart and seek the Lord.

Amy silently thanked God for leading her to Marta. What it was about this spirited young woman that moved her so she didn't know, but she had the sudden and unshakable feeling that their destinies were entwined.

CHAPTER 7

*A*nother long day at work. Another evening in an empty house. Angus sat at the table and sighed. Fleur had dropped a chicken casserole around the night before, and while part of him wanted to protest that he was quite capable of cooking for himself, he'd accepted it gratefully. The truth was that he hadn't been bothering to cook at all. It seemed pointless without Amy to share a meal with. Instead, he'd been living on microwave meals all week. So, in the end, he'd accepted the pot of food gladly and now he tucked in, wishing he had the appetite to enjoy it.

He'd been invited to Callum and Fleur's earlier to join in their film night with the kids but had declined. He was grateful for the support of his friends, but all he wanted was for his wife to come home. Attending activities alone that they would usually do together was starting to drain on his emotions, only serving to emphasise his loneliness.

He'd spoken to Amy again last night, and although he'd

been glad she sounded happier, it had worried him too. The only topic that roused any spark of life from her was when she spoke about Daisy's homeless shelter and the girl she had befriended. Angus was overjoyed that she'd found something that seemed to be lifting her out of the awful pit of depression she'd been in, but at the same time it worried him. What if she decided she was so happy there she didn't want to come home? Although he couldn't see Amy giving up her well-paying job to volunteer at a shelter full-time, a few weeks ago he would have said she would never have gone off to Melbourne without saying goodbye either. This was a side of Amy he'd never seen, and he didn't know how to navigate this uncharted emotional water.

He'd been praying for her, though, and praying hard, so he had to try and trust that whatever was going on with her would work out for the best. Maybe Marta was the medicine she needed right now.

But what about what *he* needed? He put his fork down, his appetite gone, and wondered if he should go to Callum and Fleur's after all. Sitting around here on his own wasn't going to make him feel any better.

He was clearing his plate away when the doorbell rang. He smiled to himself as he went to open it, expecting it to be Callum on a mission to persuade him to join them.

His eyes widened when he opened the door and saw that it was Cherie from the Bible study group. "Hi, can I help you?" he asked, wondering if there was anything wrong. Then he noticed the tin in her hands.

"I hope it's not a bad time. I've been thinking about what you said on Monday, and I couldn't help feeling for you. I made you a sponge cake. I hope it's not an imposition." She held the cake tin towards him.

Feeling flustered, Angus opened the door to let her in. "Not at all. It's really very kind of you. Come in." He led her into the kitchen and took the tin from her, opening the lid for a peek. It did look delicious. Sponge cake was his favourite. He felt his stomach rumble for the first time in days. Fleur's casserole was wholesome, but sponge cake, he thought wryly, was something else entirely.

He noticed Cherie looking at him eagerly. A little too eagerly, in fact. He wasn't sure what it was about her, but she made him feel uncomfortable. Nevertheless, he said, "It looks amazing. Shall I cut us a slice with some tea?"

She blushed prettily. "That sounds awesome. I'm glad you like it."

She was attractive, Angus reflected as he turned the kettle on, and perhaps it was that awareness that made him uncomfortable. Amy was away, and a woman he barely knew, whom Amy didn't know at all, was bringing him cake. He was sure she was simply lonely and looking to make friends, but it didn't feel quite right. He would have the tea and cake with her to be polite, and then make the excuse of an early night.

They made chit-chat about their day while he cut the cake and poured the tea. As he sat at the table with her, she scooted her chair closer to his. "How are you really?" she asked, her eyes wide and sympathetic.

He couldn't deny it was a relief to have someone to talk to, someone who didn't know Amy. "It's tough," he admitted. "I miss Amy and I'm trying so hard to be there for her and do the right thing, but I really just want her to come home."

"Have you asked her? Maybe she doesn't realise she's needed here."

Angus smiled ruefully. "I think she knows I want her home. But it would be selfish of me to insist on it when she's still dealing with the miscarriage. I think she simply can't face being here right now."

Cherie shook her head. "Of course, she must feel terrible after what happened. It's such a great loss. But I always think a couple in a marriage should get through things together, don't you? Support each other." She entwined her fingers together. "That's how things were for Ben and me. We did everything together."

"I'm sorry for your loss, too," Angus said softly.

She smiled. "Thank you. I know you're trying to do the right thing, but it seems very one-sided to me. After all, you're grieving, too."

Angus felt a familiar stab of frustration. She was right, even if he didn't want to admit it. There was a part of him that wanted to tell Amy she was being selfish, that his needs mattered, too. Instead, he seemed to be getting more under-standing from a woman he barely knew.

He looked at her and smiled, although he felt a great weari-ness come over him. "Amy is usually the kindest person I know," he explained, not wanting Cherie to think badly of his wife. Maybe he couldn't help but feel some resentment at her actions, but he wasn't going to discuss that with Cherie, no matter how well-meaning she might be. "I think the miscar-riage has absolutely thrown her off-kilter. I'm sure some time away will do her a world of good."

Cherie gazed at him, her eyes admiring. "You're a really

good man, I can tell. Lots of husbands wouldn't stand for it. Why, abandonment is a reason for divorce, you know." She laughed lightly as if it were a joke, but Angus grew defensive.

"She hasn't abandoned me!" *But that's how I feel,* a voice said, snaking into his mind, sliding under his skin and entwining itself around his heart, causing him to doubt himself. Was this, as he feared, the first sign that their marriage was breaking down?

No, he told himself firmly. Every couple has struggles. Amy was his soul mate. She'll come home when she's ready and they'll work through their grief together.

Yet he couldn't help conjuring up images of being without her, having to start a new life all over again. He would never divorce her, of course. He was a Christian and they'd been married in the eyes of God. He took their marriage vows seriously. But would she divorce him? *Could it really go so far?*

Cherie must have noticed his distress as she laid a comforting hand on his arm. "I'm so sorry," she said in a soothing tone. "I never should have said such a thing. I only meant that you're so very good to be so patient."

"It's all right," he said, although he didn't feel all right at all. He stood and picked up his plate. "Thank you for the cake. It really was delicious, but I think I need an early night."

"Oh." She frowned, looking disappointed. Getting up, she allowed him to walk her to the door then she turned and embraced him lightly. He stood stiffly, patting her back awkwardly. Her perfume reminded him of Amy. "I'll see you soon," she said brightly.

He nodded and smiled then closed the door after her, leaning his back against it and sighing. He felt so confused. He was sure Cherie was only being caring and kind. He would be flattering himself to assume anything else, but he couldn't shake the feeling that there'd been something inappropriate about her visit. If only Amy were here. She'd laugh at his awkwardness.

Yet he couldn't shake Cherie's words either. Was this Amy's way of leaving him and he was too naive to realise it? Plodding along on his own thinking he was giving her space while all along she was planning a new life?

Whoa buddy, he told himself, imagining Callum's voice in his head. *Calm down. It's just a few days apart.*

He wished he could fully believe that.

CHAPTER 8

*O*ver the next few days, Amy felt her fog starting to lift. Being away from home relieved her of the need to try and carry on with her usual routine in the face of her loss, and she found herself enjoying the new insights and experiences of helping at the shelter. After the feelings of uselessness and despair that had accompanied the miscarriage and her subsequent diagnosis, being at the shelter gave her a sense of purpose as well as making her feel grateful for her blessings. She enjoyed the basic kitchen work, but most of all she enjoyed listening to people and hearing their stories.

There was Al, an old alcoholic and war veteran who had fallen on hard times after his trauma from the Army had gone untreated. He struggled now to stay in one place for long, haunted by fears he would never be safe, every loud noise reminding him of the horrors he'd seen. He periodically returned to the shelter, Daisy had told her. It was one of his very few safe places, at least for certain periods.

Then there was Teresa who struggled with her mental health and was often confused, occasionally even psychotic. However, she always remembered everyone at the shelter and had a kind word for new residents.

Mike was a man in his thirties who was scarred from gang violence in his teens and had turned to drugs and crime in response to a dysfunctional upbringing and harsh environment growing up. While now drug-free and stable, he was still fighting to get permanent housing and an income, but he remained cheerful most days and took any opportunity to help out, including with the chapel.

These were the people, Amy thought, whom society had forgotten. The people others turned their faces from, not wanting to see their suffering or to examine their own consciences. But God had not forgotten them. Although not all the residents were or became Christian, and there was certainly no compulsion on them to do so, it was obvious that the simple human kindness offered at the shelter touched them all. Daisy told her that for those who did turn to God for the first time as a result of staying there, it was often through that very kindness and sense of community that the shelter offered rather than any attempt by workers and volunteers to evangelise. If anything, it was the residents who had newly become Christian who were vocal in encouraging the others. Marta was one of them.

Amy was becoming more and more fond of Marta as the week wore on. A light shone from inside her. In spite of all she'd been through, there was an innocence and idealism about her that Amy found inspirational. She'd told Amy that her own experiences had convinced her that it was her purpose to make the world a better place and help other girls who were in situations like she'd been in. Her faith and sense of purpose was humbling for Amy. While she'd always found service important, helping out at church, organising fundraisers and even going on mission when she was younger, she hadn't made it the focal point of her life like Daisy had and Marta wanted to.

But then, she'd been so certain that it was her destiny to be a mother. Everything had been geared towards that. Of course, God had blessed His children with different gifts and purposes, and Amy couldn't see herself ever being able to do what Daisy did full-time, but it had made her think about possible initiatives she could start when she returned home. Her short time at the shelter had showed her how many people needed help, not just in other countries but right here in her own environment. And while she knew that no one was saved by works, that only God's grace could save and salvation could never be earned, she also knew, to paraphrase the apostle James, that faith without works was weak.

In the sanctuary room at the shelter, Daisy had hung a framed painting of Jesus' words from the Gospel of Matthew. *'Whatsoever you do to the least of My brothers and sisters, you do also to Me.'* Next to them she'd hung the Beatitudes, a stark reminder that those in which society considered 'the least'— the poor, the sick, the prisoner and the outcast—God considered the greatest in the Kingdom of Heaven.

For the first time, Amy felt she was absorbing the true meaning and message behind the words. Being part of the community at the shelter was softening her and breaking down the armour she'd built around herself since losing the baby. While she wasn't entirely ready to confront her demons just yet, or to go home, she was getting closer with every passing day. She was praying again, and she missed Angus. So much so that she'd resolved to phone him that night and ask him to visit. She needed to see him and spend time with him away from Salford. The home she loved suddenly had become an oppressive place, although the longer she was here, the more she felt grateful for what she had. She'd never realised how many people had nowhere they could truly call home.

Marta, Daisy had told her, was in a precarious situation. While Social Services had a duty to ensure she was housed, or at least be off the streets, she would turn eighteen in a few weeks' time, and while she would be on a waiting list for housing, it could be months or even longer before she got anything. So many young people ended up on the streets in the interim while they waited for basic benefits to cover housing.

"Will she stay here while she's waiting?"

"Of course," Daisy said, "but it often means a cost for us for however long it takes for assistance to come through. We're on a shoestring really. Marta would be better placed in a youth hostel or preferably a women's refuge, but they're all full."

Amy had shaken her head at the depth of the problem and thanked God for people like Daisy who worked so tirelessly to fill the gaps in the system.

Amy let herself into the kitchen and hung her jacket on the hook. Marta was chopping vigorously on the other side of the room. "Good morning, Marta," she said cheerfully, but Marta didn't answer. Then she noticed the girl's shoulders were shaking, out of time to the jagged rhythm of her chopping.

She was crying.

"Marta? What's wrong?" Amy hurried over to her.

Marta put down the knife and wiped her eyes. When she looked at Amy, her face was twisted with despair.

Amy's breath caught in her throat. "Oh sweetheart, what's happened?"

Marta shook her head, wringing her hands in her apron. She looked almost ashamed. What on earth could have happened for her to be so distressed?

Then she dropped the bombshell. "I'm pregnant," she practically whispered, looking at Amy with tear-filled eyes.

Amy's hand flew to her mouth. "Is it...?" She stopped mid-sentence, not wanting to offend the young woman, but Marta nodded miserably.

"Yes. It can only be Steve's. I must be at least nine weeks."

Amy was frozen to the spot as a tumult of emotions rose within her. *Pregnant...Marta was pregnant.* She fought to keep the focus on the girl in front of her and remind herself that the situation must be incredibly frightening. She was so young after all, and alone. But a part of Amy screamed at the injustice and that awful, hollow feeling returned. *It's not fair.* With an effort she swallowed her feelings and took Marta's hands.

"It will be okay," she promised, speaking low and urgently. "I know you must be terribly frightened, but we'll all support you. I'm here for you, sweetheart."

Marta looked at her with an unreadable expression. "Amy, I can't...I'm not...I'm not going to have it."

Marta's words slapped her in the face like a bucket of icy water. She was so shocked that the revulsion must have shown on her face, because Marta pulled her hands away, looking hurt. Amy wanted to reassure and comfort her, but the rush of feelings overwhelmed her. Bile rose in her throat and she thought she might faint. "I have to go," she murmured, scurrying away, suddenly needing to be out of there. To be anywhere except in the kitchen with this girl who had the one thing Amy so desperately craved, and yet was boldly stating she didn't want it.

Amy scurried through the shelter, ignoring Daisy who was in conversation with a new resident, but looked up as Amy hurried past. Desperate for fresh air, Amy pushed the front door open and went outside, stumbling down the street with no idea where she was going. Her head was swimming as the emotions she'd been fighting so hard to suppress rushed up and threatened to overwhelm her.

A small park was on the corner of the road opposite. She went in and sat on a nearby bench, taking several deep breaths. Her heart hammered in her chest. She felt raw and exposed.

"Amy?"

She looked up.

Daisy was standing in front of her. "I saw you walk out. Something's upset you. What is it?"

Tears filled Amy's eyes. She couldn't hold them back any longer. Marta's news had pushed a button that had opened up all her carefully concealed feelings. "Marta's pregnant," she said bluntly, "and she doesn't want to keep the baby."

Daisy inhaled sharply. "You mean...?"

Amy nodded, feeling suddenly angry. "How can she think like that!" she blurted. "Doesn't she realise what a precious gift she's carrying?" She struggled to contain her tears and felt as if she was in a physical battle with herself.

Daisy sat down next to her, her face full of concern. "I

know this must be really hard for you to hear, given what you've just gone through," she said softly.

Nodding, Amy swiped away hot tears with the back of her hand.

"Do you think," Daisy continued in her soft voice, "that maybe Marta is just reacting out of fear? She has every right to be scared, after all."

Amy sighed. "Maybe." She now felt guilty at her immediate reaction to the girl, knowing she'd probably offended her badly. *It seems to be a pattern for me at the moment*, she thought miserably, thinking of Fleur and of course, Angus.

"Marta is young and very new to faith, too. I doubt she has much understanding of the Christian view on abortion," Daisy continued, ignoring Amy's wince at the word. Amy couldn't understand how Daisy was so unruffled about this, then remembered that in her line of work she'd seen and heard much worse than a scared young girl who had just found out she was carrying a child.

Amy sighed again, full of remorse. "I'm being horribly judgmental towards her, aren't I?"

"Perhaps," Daisy said, "but it's understandable given what you've been through. It's not Marta's fault, though, Amy, and it isn't our job as Christians to judge her. We can only guide and support her and hope that she makes the right decisions. And be here for her even if she doesn't. God is the only judge and only He can see inside the human heart. Marta has a lot of pain and conflict going on right now."

Daisy was right. Amy needed to speak to Marta and explain her actions. She looked at Daisy as tears flooded her eyes again. "Will you pray for me?" she asked.

"Of course!" Daisy exclaimed, looking on the verge of tears herself. She held Amy's hands and began to pray, her head bowed and eyes closed. "Lord God, wrap Your loving arms around Amy and heal the wounds she's been carrying for so long. Lord, show her Your mercy and compassion, and fill her with Your love. Let her know how much You love her."

Amy let out a guttural sob, then, finally unable to hold back any longer, collapsed into Daisy's arms and let the tears flow. She cried out her rage, her fear and her despair. Her feelings of resentment towards God, the world, her own body, Angus, and now, even poor Marta. Finally, she faced it all and let it go. And as she felt Daisy's comforting arms around her, she also felt the presence of the One to whom Daisy had been praying, covering her like a mother hen covers her brood. Sheltering her at her weakest.

When she'd finally finished weeping and there were no more tears left, she straightened and gratefully accepted the tissue Daisy offered.

Daisy stroked her hair gently. "Better?"

Amy nodded. She did feel better, she realised. Scrubbed out and raw, but lighter too. She walked back to the shelter arm-in-arm with Daisy. When they arrived, Marta wasn't in the kitchen.

"She's gone to her room," one of the volunteers said.

Taking a deep breath, Amy went up to Marta's room and knocked lightly on the door.

"Who is it?" The raspiness in Marta's voice suggested that she'd, too, been crying.

"It's Amy." There was a long pause and she thought Marta

was going to ignore her, but then the door opened and Marta peered out, her eyes red and puffy.

"Can I come in? I wanted to apologise and explain why I reacted the way I did."

Marta let her in wordlessly. She sat on the edge of her bed and waved Amy towards the wooden chair by the window. It was a small, sparse room with little in the way of personal possessions.

After sitting, Amy looked at Marta. She was biting her nails and regarded Amy with suspicion. Amy hadn't felt such wariness in the girl since they'd first met.

"I'm really sorry about before," she said, meaning it. "I must have seemed dismissive and judgmental." She blew out a breath. "But it was hard for me to hear. The reason I'm here staying with Daisy...well, I had a miscarriage a few weeks ago. I'd been trying for a baby for so long and it was such an awful loss. Plus, as if that wasn't enough, I found out I've got something called endometriosis, so because of that and my age, I might never be able to be a mother." She swallowed hard. "Even so, it's not an excuse for the way I behaved toward you."

Marta looked at her intently with tears in her own eyes. Amy was amazed she'd been able to articulate what she'd been going through so easily, and she knew that something had shifted inside her after talking to Daisy in the park.

"No wonder you were so upset," Marta said in a broken whisper. "I'm so sorry that happened to you."

Amy smiled sadly. "I think I'm finally coming to accept it, but it was hard to hear you talk about not wanting your baby...although I totally understand why you would feel like that."

She was determined not to push or coerce the girl in any way—Marta had experienced enough of that in her young life. She had to do as Daisy said and simply offer support. The rest was between Marta and the Lord.

"It's not that I don't want it," Marta said, looking so sad that Amy's heart broke all over again, "it's just that I don't feel I can look after it. I don't want to bring a child into the kind of mess I grew up in. I have no home, no family, and if Steve finds out..." Her lips trembled and Amy was reminded that Marta's situation was more than she could fathom.

"I'm not going to try and influence your decision in any way, Marta," Amy told her. "I know being pregnant must be terrifying for you, but I believe if you keep talking to the Lord, you'll discover what's best for you and the baby."

Marta studied her with narrowed eyes. "God would want me to keep it, wouldn't He?"

Amy thought carefully about her next words, not wanting to be judgmental again or authoritative in any way, while knowing she could only be honest about what her own faith had taught her.

"I believe, as most Christians do, that God breathes His spirit in us at the moment of conception. God knows us before we know ourselves. There's a passage in the Old Testament that tells us that God knits us together in our mother's womb, and that we are fearfully and wonderfully made."

Marta looked tearful again, but Amy also thought she could detect a glimmer of hope. "Can you show me?" She reached for the Bible by her pillow and handed it to Amy.

Amy nodded, flicked to Psalm 139 and handed it back to Marta, pointing to the lines she referred to.

Marta read them aloud slowly. "*For You formed my inmost being; You knit me together in my mother's womb. I praise You because I am fearfully and wonderfully made; Your works are wonderful, I know that full well. My frame was not hidden from You when I was made in the secret place; when I was woven together in the depths of the earth. Your eyes saw my unformed body; all the days ordained for me were written in Your book before one of them came to be.*' That's beautiful," Marta whispered, her eyes glistening.

Amy nodded. "It is. God's watching over your baby already, Marta, just as He's watching over you."

"And it means your baby is with God, too."

Amy nodded again and thought that perhaps she did have some tears left after all.

Marta crossed the room and hugged her. "Thank you," she whispered. "I still don't know what I'll do, but you've given me plenty to think about."

They embraced for a long moment before Amy told Marta to get some rest and excused herself. When she met Daisy downstairs, Daisy told her to go home. It wasn't until she reached Daisy's house and collapsed onto the couch that she realised how exhausted she was.

It was late evening when she woke. She lay on her bed for a while, her thoughts on Marta, before sitting and reaching for her Bible.

Reading through the Psalm they'd looked at in the prayer meeting, the words held even more meaning for her since opening up to Daisy. She got down on her knees and clasped her hands together, leaning on the edge of the bed.

"Lord," she murmured, "please forgive me. Forgive me for the way I reacted to Marta today. Forgive me for turning my face from You in my anger and my pain. Forgive me for being so selfish." She paused as a sense of peace slowly rose within her and assurance that she'd been heard, and her confession accepted, flowed through her. "Lord God, You are my light, my salvation and my stronghold," she continued, echoing the words of the Psalm. "May I dwell with You all my days."

She remained on her knees, drinking in the peace that truly surpasses all understanding. Out of nowhere, Angus's face appeared in her mind in striking detail, as if he were physically there before her.

Angus. A new anguish seared her heart, and in a moment all her feelings for her husband rushed in. She saw clearly how backing away must have hurt him at a time when they needed to be supporting each other. To be each other's stronghold. They'd promised, hadn't they, all those years ago, to dwell together all the days of their lives? And here she was in another city avoiding his calls. She'd only acted out of grief and beating herself up was not what the Lord wanted, but she had to put things right.

She didn't feel the need to be on her own anymore. She wanted her husband.

Getting to her feet, she rustled through her bag for her phone. She rang the house phone first, but it rang out. She glanced at the clock. Angus would usually be home from work by now, but perhaps he'd popped in to Callum and Fleur's. She knew they would be supporting him.

But when she rang his mobile, that rang out, too. She sat on the edge of the bed, phone in hand, and tried to ignore the sense of foreboding that suddenly curled in her gut.

CHAPTER 9

*A*ngus let himself into the house and hung up his coat, sighing heavily. It had been a tough day at work and coming home to an empty house was starting to get to him. Amy's missing presence was becoming almost tangible.

He'd stopped by Callum and Fleur's house after work, trying to delay the inevitable, only to feel out of place watching them sitting together happily with their children doing their homework at the table. When Fleur asked him to stay for dinner he'd politely declined, although he was hungry after having worked through his lunch break.

"If Amy isn't back in the next few days, I'll drive down and see her," Fleur said as she walked him to the front door.

Angus felt the same way himself. The only thing stopping him from driving straight to Melbourne was the fear that if he tried to push Amy into returning before she was ready, he would only succeed in pushing her away for good. Cherie's words haunted him.

He was rummaging through the kitchen cupboards trying to find something to eat when the doorbell rang. Hope leaped inside that it was Amy, even as he knew that was ridiculous. Why would she ring the doorbell to her own home?

It was Cherie. Trying to hide his disappointment, Angus smiled politely.

"I dropped by to invite you to a barbecue I'm having this weekend," she said with a chirp in her voice. She wore a floaty dress and her eyes were ringed with kohl.

"Thanks," he said, "I'll have to think about it." *But I don't have anything else going on*, he thought glumly.

Cherie seemed to sense how he was feeling. Cocking her head to one side, she smiled sympathetically. "Would you like some company? You look how I feel."

He held the door open. She was empathetic. In that regard, she reminded him of Amy.

She followed him into the kitchen. He fixed them both a drink then leaned against the counter while she sat at the breakfast bar.

"So, how are you? Any more word from your wife?"

"We've spoken. She's doing better." He shrugged. Although Cherie was kind, he didn't want to discuss Amy with her in any depth. He already felt he'd said too much the other night. Cherie seemed to sense that and began to make chit-chat about her day, then asked him about his. As Angus told her about his work at Salford's renewable energy firm and his passion for sustainability, Cherie listened intently. He couldn't help but think how long it had been since Amy had given him this level of undivided attention, although he immediately felt disloyal at the thought. Even so, it was flattering how genuinely interested Cherie seemed.

He heard a warning bell in his head but pushed it to one side, telling himself not to be uncharitable. She was a nice woman and it was only Christian to be hospitable.

But then she scooted towards him on her chair. Since his back was in the corner and he couldn't move away, he realised how close they were.

He stopped talking, suddenly uncomfortable with the way she was gazing at him.

"Your job sounds so interesting," she said, and suddenly, before Angus understood what she was about to do, she stood and brushed her lips against his.

"Whoa!" he exclaimed, pushing her away more roughly than he'd intended in his sudden panic. She tripped over the stool, and he helped to right her only for her to push herself against him again.

"Let us comfort each other," she whispered. "We're both alone."

He held her at arm's length firmly but more gently this time and stepped out of the corner and away from her. When he released her, her face went blank and she hung her head. He felt awful. *I've been such a fool,* he told himself sternly. *I should never have let her in.*

"Cherie," he said firmly but not without compassion. "I'm a married man and I love my wife. I'm sorry if I gave you the impression otherwise. It certainly was not my intention. I'm afraid I'm going to have to ask you to leave."

She nodded, unable to meet his gaze. Stains of scarlet

appeared on her cheeks and he felt sorry for her as she rushed past him and left the house without speaking.

Angus rubbed a hand over his jaw, sighing heavily. He should have seen this coming, he thought wearily. Instead, he'd been flattered by the attention and the offer of friendship and let loneliness blind him to what should have been obvious. Now she'd made a fool of herself and he felt terrible. And guilty. What on earth would Amy say if she knew? She'd have every right to be furious with him as much as with Cherie.

Amy. Suddenly overcome with longing for his wife, he reached in his pocket for his phone then realised he must have left it in the car. He hurried out to get it, checking first that Cherie wasn't lingering.

His phone was on the passenger seat, flashing that he had three missed calls. They were all from Amy. She'd been trying to call him when he'd been in their house talking to another woman who clearly had more than friendship on her mind. His hands shaking, he called back, but this time she didn't answer. Perhaps she went to bed early.

He stared into the sky for several moments, then made up his mind. Without bothering to get changed or gather his things, he jogged back to the house and locked the front door then got back into the car and revved the engine.

He was going to find his wife.

THE WHOLE WAY TO MELBOURNE, Angus prayed incessantly that it wouldn't be too late, and that Amy had been phoning because she missed him and wanted to come home and not for any other reason. He thought about the fear that Cherie had planted in his mind, perhaps not unintentionally, and realised it had been largely irrational. Amy had just needed time away, understandable after the emotional and physical turmoil she'd suffered, and he'd let himself succumb to emotional insecurities and accusations. No wonder Cherie had assumed he would be responsive to her advances. They hadn't even been particularly subtle, he realised.

Lord forgive me, he prayed as he drove. *I've been so blind. I've given into fear instead of trusting You. Help Amy and me to find our way back to each other again.*

He thought of the sermon that had been preached at their wedding. The pastor had spoken about the need to treat marriage like a precious jewel, something to be both treasured and guarded. By letting Cherie in when he was alone, he'd not been guarding the sanctity of their marriage. Even if his intentions had never been anything untoward, he nevertheless had left an opening for Cherie to try and exploit. Although he did feel sorry for the woman—she was clearly lonely and confused —she was not his priority. Amy was. Angus prayed that Amy would forgive him, just as he knew God had.

Lord, keep our marriage under Your precious protection, he prayed, suddenly acutely aware of the cross he wore around his neck, tucked into the collar of his shirt. *Help us to turn towards each other instead of away.*

He had to confess to Amy. He couldn't let her return without knowing that he'd almost allowed another woman into his life, albeit with the best of intentions. Honesty and integrity had always been the touchstones of both their relationship and their attempts to live out their faith in the world. He prayed that she would forgive him.

Although he'd tried his best to be supportive, he'd also tried to take on the role of Amy's rescuer, caring for her through her grief while avoiding his own. Perhaps if they'd grieved together and he'd been more open about the fact that he too was heartbroken about the baby, then maybe the chasm between them wouldn't have grown so wide. It had been so much easier to worry about safeguarding Amy's feelings than attempting to process his own.

With that realisation, Angus fully surrendered, giving every last drop of his pain and anguish to God, welcoming Him into his heart with as much fervour as he had when he was younger and had first found his faith. As he drove towards Melbourne, tears filled his eyes.

CHAPTER 10

*A*my had just stepped out of the shower and was about to blow dry her hair when she heard a loud and urgent knocking at the door. Wrapping her robe around herself, she went to see what was going on. From the top of the stairs she heard Daisy open the door and greet someone in surprise, then she heard a voice that made her heart sing.

Angus.

She ran down the stairs and stopped at the bottom. Stared at him. He looked flustered and she sensed there was something wrong, but then he opened his arms and she ran into them, laying her head on his chest. From the corner of her eye she saw Daisy smile and quietly retreat into the lounge and shut the door behind her, giving them privacy.

Amy nestled into the strong arms of her husband. Breathed in the scent of him. Listened to his heartbeat. Now that he was here, she completely realised what she'd been missing in her self-imposed exile.

He buried his face in her hair and held her as though he was frightened to ever let her go again.

Amy gazed up at him with moist eyes and pressed her lips against his, reminding herself of his familiar taste and the contours of his mouth. Her husband. Her love. "I'm sorry," she whispered. "I should never have left like I did."

He shook his head. Gazed into her eyes. "You did what you needed to do. I should have been more understanding."

They gazed at each other for a few minutes, drinking each other in, then Amy took his hand. "Let's go upstairs to talk. Daisy's watching TV in the lounge."

Angus followed her up, hands securely on her waist. Reaching her room, they sat next to each other on her bed. He took her hands in his. "I'm sorry to turn up like this, but I had to see you, Amy."

She smiled. "I'm so glad you did. I tried to phone you earlier because I had to see *you*. Something happened today...it helped me realise that I can't keep hiding."

Angus stroked her palm with his thumb. "Tell me what happened." His voice was soft and soothing. Comforting.

She told him about Marta and how quickly she'd formed a bond with the young woman, and then about her reaction to Marta's news and the unleashing of emotion it had triggered. She was wiping tears away again when she finished.

Emotion flickered across his face as he lifted her hand to his lips and kissed it gently. "It sounds like God brought you two together. If something good comes out of our loss, if it can help this young girl make the right decision, then at least our suffering hasn't been in vain."

Amy nodded, and although she thoroughly agreed, she also knew that Angus was a great one for using platitudes to cover up his own feelings.

"You're right, but how do *you* feel, Angus? I've been so wrapped up in my own grief that I completely neglected the fact that the loss of our baby affected you, too. I'm so sorry."

He squeezed her hand, whether in reassurance or gratitude she wasn't sure. "I suppose it was easier for me to concentrate on you than look at my own feelings. I didn't want to face how hurt I've been, too. It felt like all our dreams and hopes had been dashed, and I felt so helpless in the face of it all. It wasn't something I could fix or negotiate or manage."

They clung to each other, then Amy said in a small voice, "Part of the reason I left was because I felt I wasn't good enough, knowing that I might never be able to give you a child. In my self-pity, I convinced myself you'd be better off without me."

Angus's eyes widened. "Amy, I love you! That hasn't changed. If anything, I've realised all over again just how much I do. It's disappointing if we can't have children, and I know how painful that would be for you—for both of us—but we're in this together. You're my wife." He traced her hairline gently with the tip of his fingers.

She smiled through tears and kissed him on the cheek. "I knew that, deep down, but I couldn't see straight. I even convinced myself you would be better off with someone else who can give you children." She laughed, but when Angus responded with a grimace, she felt a sudden twist in her gut. Something was wrong. "What is it?" she asked.

He let out a heavy sigh. "I need to tell you something. Nothing happened and never would have. I'm completely and forever committed to our marriage. But I've been foolish."

"What are you talking about?" she asked, frowning as she recalled the sense of foreboding she'd felt earlier. Panic welled within her.

She listened with alarm as Angus told her about Cherie, shaking her head in disbelief when he told her about the woman's visit earlier that evening. "Surely when she turned up again you must have realised her intentions?"

He shook his head glumly. "Not really. Maybe deep down I knew something was wrong and her behaviour was inappropriate, but I didn't want to be unkind. And if I'm totally honest, I was lonely, and I suppose it was company of a sort."

"You have plenty of friends, Angus," Amy snapped, pulling away from him. Although she believed that he'd never had any bad intentions, she also felt bitterly hurt that he entertained another woman in their house. A woman they barely knew. Amy thought she'd seen her at church, but she'd never said more than 'hello' to her. And she was on her doorstep as soon as she was off the scene! Jealousy seethed inside her.

"I know. My actions were inexcusable. I haven't been thinking straight all week." He grabbed her hands and looked deep into her eyes. "But Amy, nothing happened nor would it have. You do believe me?"

She felt herself soften a little. She did believe him. All these years of marriage, she knew her husband. She'd always been the only woman he'd ever wanted, going right all the way back to college when he'd been too shy to speak to her. "I believe you," she said quietly. "I just wish you'd been more mindful of what you were doing. Letting her in was a mistake and obviously gave her completely the wrong idea."

"I feel so stupid now," he murmured. "Can you forgive me, Amy?"

She bit her lip. She couldn't deny she was still angry, and she would have to fight the urge to give this Cherie a piece of her mind when she returned, but she couldn't hold it against him when he was obviously blaming himself more than she ever could. She reached up and stroked his cheek, taking in his handsome face. "Of course I do. And can you forgive me for taking off like I did? Neither of us has been perfect here."

"There's nothing to forgive," he whispered, leaning down to kiss her again, enfolding her in his arms. She relaxed into his strength as she thanked God for bringing them back to each other.

He stroked her hair, and with each touch it was as though he was stroking her fears and anxieties away. Peace settled over her and she felt an intense surge of gratitude for the goodness of the Lord.

"Can we pray together?" she said.

He nodded and smiled. "That's a great idea, my love. Let me read Psalm twenty-seven to you first. We've been looking at it in Bible study and it's been such a comfort these past few days."

Amy chuckled in delight. "Really? We read it at the shelter, too. And yes, it's beautiful, but like all the Psalms, so raw and real."

They both shook their heads at the coincidence and Amy smiled at the thought of them both reading the same scripture and deriving comfort from it even while they had been so far apart.

"Let's read it together," she suggested and then picked up her Bible. As they read it together, line by line, Amy reflected on how it made the words take on new meaning. No reading of Scripture was ever the same twice. The Word was a living, breathing text that held infinite meaning, and yet somehow also spoke precisely to her daily reality. As they read through the Psalm, she thought about how she and Angus together were a stronghold against the enemy, and how their marriage could be a dwelling place for the Spirit so long as they both kept their faces turned towards the Lord. She'd been so silly to think she would be better off without him.

She was about to voice her thoughts aloud in prayer when Angus suddenly looked both excited and apprehensive at the same time, as though something had just startled him. "I've just had a thought, or rather, the thought had me," he said.

"What is it?" Amy asked, intrigued. She knew that such things were so often the urgings of the Holy Spirit and not to be ignored.

"This Marta girl, she obviously means a lot to you?"

Amy smiled sadly. "Yes, she does." She couldn't explain exactly what it was about her, but Amy felt both a deep connection and the overwhelming urge to nurture her.

"And she has to leave the shelter?"

Amy shook her head. "Daisy won't kick her out before she has a place to go to, but the shelter is designed to be temporary housing. Now that Marta's pregnant, I'm not sure what will happen. It could take some time for her and the baby—*if* she has the baby—to get housed." Amy shuddered as she thought of the girl's difficult predicament.

"What about the group home over on the other side of Salford? Our church has links with it, I'm sure."

Amy sat bolt upright. Angus was right. The group home for vulnerable women in Salford, aptly named Hope House, could be the perfect solution for Marta until she got on her feet.

Now that he'd mentioned it, it was so obvious Amy couldn't believe it hadn't occurred to her earlier. "You're right. I'll speak to her about it tomorrow."

As she snuggled back into his arms, tiredness washed over her. It had been a long and emotional day. "Are you staying?" she asked, lifting her face.

Angus kissed her forehead. "Well, I wasn't planning on driving all the way back to Salford tonight," he chuckled. "I can take tomorrow off work. I have some time in lieu I can use."

"You should come to the shelter." Amy yawned. "Meet Marta."

"I'd like that," Angus said.

Slipping into bed, Amy laid her head on his chest, stroking the familiar contours of his stomach. She remembered early in their marriage when they had lain like this for hours, talking and setting the world to rights, back in the days when they were still young enough to believe no adversity could touch them. Amy knew now that adversity was part of life, but that as long as she had her faith, she could get through anything.

And as long as she and Angus had each other, things were ultimately good in her world. "I love you," she murmured, her fingertips tracing circles across his torso. She felt her eyelids drooping as the day caught up with her.

"I love you, too, Amy" Angus replied, and she heard the truth in his words.

Resting in each other's arms, all their cares were forgotten for a few blissful moments before sleep claimed them.

CHAPTER 11

The next morning when Angus and Amy headed downstairs, the aroma of freshly brewed coffee and croissants filled the air.

Daisy was already sitting at the breakfast table sipping coffee. She looked up and smiled. "Have you got plans for the day? You're both welcome to stay as long as you like."

Amy glanced at Angus and then back at Daisy. "Angus has taken the day off, so I thought I'd take him to the shelter to meet Marta." A smile tugged at her lips. "He had an idea last night."

When Angus explained about Hope House, Daisy beamed with delight. "That's a wonderful idea. Assuming she agrees, of course and there is a free space."

Amy nodded enthusiastically. "It could make a real difference to her." She held Angus's hand under the table before continuing. "It's been lovely staying here and helping out at the shelter, and I can't thank you enough for having me, Daisy, but I think I'll be going back to Salford tonight."

Angus blinked and stared at her. "You're coming home?"

Amy smiled shyly. "Assuming you still want me to."

A broad smile spread across his face. "Of course I do. But," his smile faded, "are you sure you're ready?"

"As much as I'll ever be." She felt nervous, but if she didn't return to normality and face everyday life now, it wasn't going to get any easier. The last few days had taught her a lot about herself and helped her face the things she'd been running from, but now it was time to go home. "Besides," she added, "it sounds like you need protection from Cherie."

Daisy frowned. "Who's Cherie?"

Angus groaned and put his head in his hands.

Although Amy kept her tone light as she relayed the story, a small amount of jealousy and anger pinched at her. It was an uncomfortable, gnawing feeling.

Daisy reached over the table and took her other hand, seemingly sensing Amy's strong emotion. "She sounds like a very unhappy woman," she said softly. "That doesn't mean you can't feel angry. As for you, Angus," she said sternly but with a twinkle in her eye, "could you be any denser?"

Angus sighed as he slipped his arm around Amy's shoulders. "I know, I know," he said wearily, still looking mortified. "I should have known better."

As Amy smiled at him, her anger melted away. One of the reasons she'd fallen for her husband in the first place was his humility, and she knew it was precisely that humbleness that stopped him from realising Cherie's motives. He had an ability to always see the best in people and try to be a gentleman, which was a strength but also the source of rare naivety.

They got ready and walked to the shelter with Daisy, Angus plying her with questions about the residents and how the shelter worked. Daisy chatted with him easily while Amy whispered a prayer of gratitude. She still felt very raw and fragile, but her hope and optimism were gradually being restored.

She thought of Marta and said a prayer for her, too, hoping that their conversation the day before and the verses they'd read together might have moved the girl enough for her to at least start to reconsider her original plan.

At the same time, Amy knew it wouldn't help for her to react badly again, so she also prayed for God to give her a spirit of non-judgment. Finally, she asked God to soften Marta's heart.

When they arrived at the shelter, Marta was sitting with one of the short-stay residents and going through a government assistance form with her. Amy smiled to see how the girl was so intent on helping others even though she certainly had her own challenges right now. When Marta saw her, she smiled, said something to the other resident, and then came over. There was a look on her face that Amy couldn't quite place. Slightly anxious yet determined.

"This is my husband, Angus." Amy introduced them to each other, noticing how Marta appraised Angus, and then she gave a small nod. Her eyes were glistening when she asked Amy, "Can I talk to you?"

"Of course."

She left Angus with Daisy and stepped into the sanctuary

with Marta who shut the door behind them and then turned to face her. "I have something to tell you."

Amy braced herself.

"After the scripture you showed me yesterday...well, I prayed all night and you're right. My baby deserves her life. Don't ask me how," she said with a shy smile, "but I just know she's a girl."

Relief surged through Amy and she smiled, unable to keep the joy from her voice. "I'm so glad, Marta. If there's anything I can do to help...in fact..." She started to tell Marta about Hope House, but Marta cut in, her words coming in a rush.

"The thing is, I'm not in a place in my own life to give her the life I would want her to have, so I've decided to have her adopted. But I don't want to spend forever worrying that she's not with the right family...so, I want you and your husband to have her."

Amy gasped. Blinked.

Marta's eyes filled with tears. "Please, I know it's a lot to ask, but don't answer yet. Promise me you'll think about it?" She was pleading now, her eyes wide and beseeching.

Amy stood rooted to the spot, not knowing how to feel or react. Marta's suggestion had taken her by surprise but filled her with anticipation. Finally, she nodded. "I don't know what to say, Marta. This is such a shock. I'll have to think about it. And pray about it."

Marta flung herself into Amy's arms and as Amy returned the hug, she realised once more how slight the girl was.

"I know you're the right person. I really believe God brought us together for this moment."

Amy nodded slowly, feeling the truth of Marta's words. She

pulled away and met Marta's gaze. "I need to speak to Angus, and I can't make any promises, but let's talk seriously about this, okay?" Then she remembered Hope House. "I don't know if this might change how you feel, but we've thought of somewhere that might be more suitable for you to stay."

When Amy explained about Hope House, Marta's outlook lifted further.

Returning to the main reception, Angus raised his brow inquiringly. "Are you okay, Amy?"

Was she okay? She felt strangely disembodied and not entirely sure how she felt. She smiled weakly. "Let's go for a walk," she murmured, taking his arm and leading him out of the shelter.

CHAPTER 12

One month later...

*A*my collapsed onto Fleur's couch with a sigh and gratefully accepted the Earl Grey her friend held out to her. She'd taken the day off work to help Marta move from the shelter into Hope House. It had been more work than she'd expected. Thanks to the generosity of others, Marta had moved into her new home with more belongings than she'd arrived at the shelter with, and Amy had insisted on carrying everything, ever mindful of the girl's condition.

The pre-adoption process was underway. It was looking promising that she and Angus would be accepted, and that Marta's baby would be placed with them once born. It had all happened so quickly that Amy often felt overwhelmed, and today was no exception. Fleur sat next to her on the couch, tucking her legs to the side. "Did she get settled in okay?"

Amy nodded, smiling as she remembered Marta's excited face as she saw her new home. It was a beautiful town house on the other side of Salford that she would share with five other women and a house mother who lived in during the week. She would receive support with finances, education, and the eventual move into independent living. And of course, with her spiritual journey. Although being Christian was not a requirement for women to use the service, many of those who went through Hope House found that the Lord revealed Himself to them as part of their journey. Marta, of course, already had a strong faith and Amy had no doubt she would soon be sharing that faith with the other residents.

"Yes, I think she'll really enjoy it there. And it's easier for all of us to have her closer, you know, for appointments and stuff."

Fleur nodded, taking a sip of her tea.

Amy thought back to Marta's first scan a fortnight ago. Amy had gone with her and felt a strange mixture of both excitement, apprehension, and a stab of grief that she'd never gotten to see her own baby that way. As if sensing her thoughts, Marta had held her hand and squeezed it, rather than the other way around. Although Marta had shown relief that the baby was well, she hadn't shown any sign of regretting her decision when she'd seen the tiny form on the screen. She seemed to be completely determined.

It was a worry of Amy's, of course, that Marta would change her mind and decide she didn't want to give her baby to Amy and Angus after all. She certainly couldn't blame the girl if she did, and Amy often wrestled with herself, wondering if she was doing the wrong thing by taking a baby from its birth mother. Since neither Marta nor Angus seemed to share her concerns, she tried to swallow her doubts and concentrate on the fact that she would soon be a mother after all, even if not quite in the way she'd expected. Marta never expressed anything but delight that her baby would grow up in a stable family home. That was her focus, and the girl regularly thanked Amy with effusiveness, showing no sign of having second thoughts. But she had almost six months of pregnancy left, and Amy couldn't help but think Marta might change her mind when the baby started kicking.

Angus had taken an entirely pragmatic approach throughout. When she had initially told him about Marta's suggestion, he'd been surprised but not as shocked as she'd expected. After some time in quiet reflection and prayer, he'd agreed that it was the ideal situation and that Marta had indeed been placed on their path by God. The coincidences were too many for them to ignore.

Amy wasn't sure why she felt so uncertain, even though it was what she wanted. She would love the baby as if it were her own. Neither would Marta be left out. Both she and Angus agreed that Marta should play a part in the baby's life. Yet something worried her.

She voiced her concerns to Fleur, who listened and then said in a soft voice, "Do you think it's fear? That you'll get your hopes and dreams up only to have them dashed again?"

Exhaling loudly, Amy nodded. As usual, Fleur had hit the nail perfectly on its head. She didn't want to admit it because she was trying so hard to trust in God's plan, but yes, she feared making plans again only for them not to materialise. From the moment they'd agreed to the adoption to the day of Marta's scan, Amy had felt as though she were holding her breath, praying that this scan would show a whole and healthy baby.

"Yes, I think that's it," she said. "I keep thinking, no, of course nothing will go wrong. It's so obvious that God has His hand in this, but then, who knows? I try not to think of all the things that could go wrong..." Her voice trailed off, not wanting to delve into all her fears and give them any more power.

Fleur smiled, her eyes filled with empathy. "I know it's a different situation, but I can't help thinking of how frightened I was when I met Callum and found out he knew Jeff, then he was called up that last time. I felt the same way. Torn between trusting God when it was so obvious we were destined to meet, and tormenting myself with all the things that could go wrong."

Amy nodded, remembering her friend's predicament and glad she understood her turmoil.

"And do you remember what you said to me?" Fleur asked, brow cocked.

Amy chuckled. "No, but I'm sure you're about to repeat it to me."

"Of course!" Fleur laughed, nudging her friend playfully. "I remember you told me it was only natural to be afraid, that I was only human. You suggested that if I try and remember that, along with keeping my faith in God, it would all work out."

Amy smiled and shook her head. "I said that? I was quite

wise, wasn't I?"

"Yes, you were, but I suppose it's always easier to be wiser about other people's problems than it is your own. And sometimes waiting is hard. Waiting on the Lord is hard. Try to remember this—He always delivers. The promised land is ahead, but sometimes we have to keep trudging."

"I know." Amy sighed heavily. "It's just that sometimes I feel like we've waited so long and been trying for a baby for so many years that I simply don't have the strength in me for this final mile."

"But you do," Fleur said, rubbing her arm. "And deep down you know you do. You're one of the strongest people I know. And when you don't have the strength—because let's face it, we all have those days—those are the times you need to lean on the Lord. Let Him be your strength, your rock and your refuge. Doesn't it say that in the Psalm you have on your wall?"

Amy nodded. "Psalm twenty-seven." Simply remembering the beautiful words soothed her. After she and Angus realised they'd both been praying on it while apart, she'd had it printed on canvas and hung it in their living room once arriving home. It had become 'their' Psalm. Although she had a tinge of jealousy when Angus told her it had been Cherie who'd read it out at the Bible study group. Perhaps there'd been a purpose to even that, Amy had decided, refusing to let one person's bad actions overshadow her peace.

As if reading her mind, Fleur changed the subject—right on to Cherie. "I saw Cherie yesterday. You know she's dating Richard Hughes now?"

Amy's brows lifted. Richard was their church's most infamous bachelor. "Well, I hope they're both happy," she said and realised she meant it. Facing Cherie once she'd come home had been difficult when she'd so wanted to give the woman a piece of her mind, but when she and Angus had seen her at church the following Sunday, she'd looked so mortified that Amy couldn't help feeling sorry for her. Cherie had kept her distance ever since and even changed her Bible study group, which Amy had been grateful for.

"Yes, me too. It seems like the perfect pairing, somehow," Fleur agreed.

They sat in comfortable, silent reflection for a few moments before Amy finished her tea and got to her feet. "I'd better get going, it's my turn to cook. Would you, Callum, and the kids like to come for dinner on Saturday? We've invited Marta and I thought it would be nice for her to meet you all properly."

Fleur gave an enthusiastic nod. "We'd love to," she said as she walked Amy to the door.

Amy drove home and started to prepare dinner, a wave of gratitude for her friends and family washing over her. She and Angus were closer than ever after her stay at Daisy's. It was as though they'd both had to confront their emotional barriers and hit the proverbial rock bottom before they'd surrendered. She'd never felt so close to her husband, or so in love.

Whatever happened, she thought as she glanced up at the canvas on the wall, she knew that this time they would get through it together.

CHAPTER 13

Four Months Later

ngus checked the time on the dashboard of his car. He was early. Clipping off his belt, he reclined his seat a fraction to relax while waiting for Marta. Although the local vocational college wasn't far from Hope House, she was nearly eight months pregnant and he wasn't about to let her walk. Although pregnancy had filled her out, she still had that fragile, almost waif-like appearance about her, and recently she'd been looking especially exhausted, the weight of the child taking its toll on her young body.

The child. With the birth so near, he and Amy had begun making plans. The nursery was decorated, although Amy had insisted on not putting the cot up until they were ready to bring the baby home. Marta had requested they call her Angel, which both he and Amy had thought was simply perfect. The adoption process had gone through and all that remained was for the papers to be signed when the baby was born.

Of course, either they or Marta could change their mind when Angel was finally here. Amy was becoming increasingly worried about this. Late at night when they lay in each other's arms, she shared her worries with him.

"I know she still talks about the adoption in positive terms," Amy had said the previous night, her voice a whisper. "But I can see she's starting to bond with her. When she thinks I'm not looking, all she does is stroke her stomach. And she told me she sings to the baby. She read in a magazine that Angel can hear her voice from the inside."

"Isn't that a good thing?" Angus had asked, trying to reassure her. "Angel will be having the best possible start, absorbing all that love. Marta doesn't want us to have her because she doesn't care for her, but precisely because she *does*. She knows we can give Angel a better life and she'll always be able to see her."

They'd even made plans for Marta to stay with them for the first few weeks after Angel's birth so they could transition gradually and make sure Angel received all the contact needed for her attachment instincts to develop as they should. It seemed to Angus that they'd covered every angle, but he was looking at this through practical eyes. The bonds that were being forged between Marta, Angel, and Amy were ones he knew he could never tangibly share, even though he was as invested in this as Amy. But he wanted things to work out, too.

In fact, although he didn't want to voice his fears to Amy at such a precarious time, he worried about what it would do to her if things didn't turn out as planned. To have her dreams dashed again would push her to the limit. He'd already determined, however, that this time they'd get through any problems together, not apart.

Since Amy had returned to Salford their marriage had grown stronger and stronger. Going through such a difficult time, as harrowing as it had been, had only strengthened them in the longer term.

And Marta had become a part of the family. She'd come over for dinner twice a week and she and Amy had grown close. Fleur and Callum loved her, as did Fleur's kids. They'd all become the family Marta had never had. Angus wondered how that would change when Angel was born. Would Marta realistically be able to spend so much time with them all after giving birth, watching another woman raise her baby? Angus knew that was another one of Amy's fears...that they would keep Angel but lose Marta. There seemed to be so many variables that none of them had considered when this arrangement had first been agreed to.

God's hand is in this, Angus reminded himself. They needed to concentrate on that and have faith. God had led them through the dark places, all three of them, and brought them all together for Angel's sake, of that he had no doubt. Amy was simply getting jittery now that the time was drawing closer. Just over a month and little Angel would be here.

It would be easier to reassure himself of that if Marta had not been subdued recently, and the more he thought about it, the more he was unconvinced it was plain tiredness. These last two weeks, she hadn't come around to their home as often as she normally did, and when she did come, she was much quieter. Even withdrawn.

Not that she was ever loud. Marta had settled in at Hope House and made friends with the residents, but she still retained that air of aloofness, of keeping to herself. She was studying a pre-vocational course at the technical and further education centre so she could achieve her dreams of studying Social Work after Angel was born. She wanted to be a youth worker, working with young people and offenders. Angus thought she'd be great at it. But she hadn't made any strong friends at college. Although she was always friendly and personable, it was as if there was a visible barrier around the girl, keeping everyone at arm's length. If the only person who'd ever penetrated that barrier was Amy, then perhaps they were right to worry about the effect on her when Amy was raising her daughter. Angus knew that Amy's biggest fear for Marta, although she wouldn't voice it, was that she would return to her old life after having her baby.

Angus looked up as he saw Marta in his side mirror, emerging from the building across the road. She glanced around but didn't see him because of the van parked behind him. He was about to call out to her when she took her phone from her pocket and put it to her ear, turning away as if to shield herself. There was something about her demeanour and expression that gave Angus pause. Something secretive. She wasn't looking for him to be there so much as checking he wasn't. His stomach lurched. The only person Marta wouldn't want to be seen talking to was Steve, her ex.

Marta rarely spoke about him or addressed the fact that he was Angel's father. She'd been adamant about putting 'father unknown' on the birth certificate to stop him turning up and blocking the adoption if he found out about Angel. Surely she'd experienced too many horrors at his hands to give him the time of day now. Angus shook his head, chiding himself for being so suspicious, and leaned out the car door.

"Marta!" he called. "Over here!"

When she glanced up, he didn't miss the sudden panic that crossed her face or the way she snapped her phone shut and shoved it back into her pocket. She crossed quickly and slid into the car awkwardly. Her stomach was large under her hoodie, although the rest of her body remained as slender as a whippet.

"How was your day?" he asked as he pulled away from the kerb.

"It was okay," she answered. "We did statistics so it was a bit boring. But it's stuff I need to know, I suppose." She seemed distracted, twisting a lock of hair round her finger.

"Who was on the phone?" Angus asked, trying to sound as nonchalant as possible but failing miserably.

Marta glanced at him and he saw her stiffen. "Oh, I was just checking the time of my next midwife appointment," she said casually. *Too casually.*

Angus nodded and kept his eyes on the road, but suspicion and worry curled around his stomach.

When he dropped Marta off at Hope House, he made a point of walking her in. After a brief goodbye, she went straight to her room. He realised she hadn't even asked after Amy, which wasn't like her at all. There could be no doubt she was acting oddly.

When he heard her door shut, he knocked softly on the

door of the house mother's room. The kindly middle-aged woman opened it, giving him a wide smile that faded. Obviously, she noted his brow furrowed in concern and the downward turn of his lips.

"Can I have a word?" he asked quietly.

"Of course. Come in, Angus." She shut the door behind them and looked at him expectantly.

He cleared his throat. "I was wondering how Marta's getting on and if you've noticed anything different of late."

When the woman nodded, Angus felt his stomach sink even further.

"Just the last week or so," she said. "She's not been engaging as much. Hasn't even come to Bible study, and you know that Marta is usually so committed. It's almost as if her light is fading. I thought it was just that her pregnancy's progressing, and God knows the last few months are hard work, but..." She hesitated, wringing her hands together, seemingly unsure as to whether she should speak about what was clearly on her mind.

"But?" Angus prompted anxiously.

"Well, I'm sure I've heard her talking on the phone late at night a few times. It might be nothing, but..."

"You think she's talking to her ex." Angus finished the sentence for her. He ran a hand through his hair, exhaling loudly.

"I think it's a possibility."

"But wasn't the guy terrible to her?"

The house mother sighed heavily. "Yes. And I know it seems completely counterintuitive that she could ever go back, but I've been doing this sort of work for a long time and I've seen it happen over and over again. These men get into the heads of vulnerable young women who are often no more than children, and it can take a long, long time to get them out again. He might have been the very devil himself to her, but he's also the only man to ever show her love. You can't imagine the damage that can do to a vulnerable young mind."

Angus didn't know what to say, but he felt desperately sad.

"I know you and your wife have been good to her," the woman said, "but sometimes these girls have to do a lot of wrestling with their demons—very real demons—before they can really break free." *If they ever do* was the unspoken ending to that sentence.

"Should I say something to her?" Angus asked, feeling at a loss for what to do.

The house mother shook her head. "No, we're only surmising at the moment. I'm due to have a chat with her in the morning. I conduct a private support session with all the women once a week. I'll raise it then."

Angus nodded. That was probably a better approach. He had no idea what to say in this situation and felt completely out of his depth, though his heart ached for Marta. "Can you phone me in the morning after you've spoken to her? I won't say anything to Amy yet."

"I think that's best," the woman said soothingly. "Go home and pray for her."

Angus nodded. That was the least he could do.

When he arrived home, Amy had already finished work and was sitting on the couch, knitting. She'd taught herself to knit over the last few months and Angel was going to have more knitted bonnets, cardigans and bootees than any baby could possibly know what to do with. When he walked in, she put her knitting down, jumped up, and hugged him. He put his arms around her, inhaling her familiar scent and thinking once again how much he adored this woman. His fears eased a little as she kissed him then turned to show him what she was working on.

He looked blankly at the latest mass of wool. "It doesn't seem to have much shape yet," he said, wondering where the sleeves were.

"That's because it's a *blanket*, Angus," she said with a chuckle. Then her eyes narrowed. "Something's wrong. Is it work?"

"Everything's fine," he said, but then he sighed. He was rubbish at lying. "I'm sure it's nothing, but Marta seems so subdued." He was reluctant to tell Amy about the phone call he'd witnessed.

Amy sat back on the couch, nodding. "I mentioned that last night."

"I know," he said as he sat next to her and took her hand. "I spoke to the house mother when I dropped her off, and she's noticed it, too. She's due to have a support session with Marta tomorrow and she said she'll raise it with her then. She'll let us know if there's anything to be worried about."

"And the rest?"

Angus looked at her blankly.

"I know when you're trying to protect me," she said with a wry smile. "What is it?"

He let out a heavy breath and reluctantly told her about the phone calls the house mother suspected were to Marta's ex.

Amy covered her face with her hands before finally looking at him, her face ashen. "I knew something was wrong." Her voice hitched and she sounded as if she were about to cry.

Angus took her hands and gently stroked them. "It might be nothing, but we should pray for her. Have you spoken to her today?"

"Briefly this morning. She seemed okay and said she'd be over for dinner tomorrow."

"We're probably worrying about nothing, then," Angus said with more conviction than he felt.

"Maybe. Let's have dinner, then we can spend some time praying for her."

Angus nodded in agreement, surprised at Amy's calmness despite her obvious concern. He realised he didn't always give his wife credit for the strength she possessed.

After dinner, they held hands and prayed for Marta.

"Heavenly Father," Amy began, her voice clear with conviction, "we know that You're watching over Marta and Angel and that they're so precious to You. Please help Marta to know in herself how precious she is and to feel Your presence surrounding her and Your arms enfolding her. Whatever is on her mind, may it be eased. May she be guided ever to seek Your face and not to succumb to doubt, despair or temptation. Give her strength and courage. In Jesus' name. Amen."

"Amen," Angus echoed and then continued with a prayer of his own. "Lord, thank You for all You've done for our family and for Marta and Angel. Thank You for leading us out of the darkness and into new hope and new life. Whatever Marta is going through right now, we pray that she's able to hold on to her faith and know that You are with her. In the valley and on the mountaintop. Amen."

"Amen." Amy looked up with tear-filled eyes. They sat and embraced for a long moment before going upstairs to bed.

AFTER A NIGHT of Amy tossing and turning in a fitful sleep while Angus held her and tried to soothe her while struggling to sleep himself, the worry continued no matter how much he tried to turn his thoughts to prayer.

He was still on his back, staring at the ceiling, when the phone rang. He glanced at the clock and his heart sank. Six a.m. At that hour in the morning it could only be bad news.

Praying he was wrong, he gently slipped his arm out from underneath Amy, who'd finally fallen asleep, and hurried downstairs to answer the phone. "Hello," he said tentatively.

"Angus?" It was the house mother from Hope House, and she sounded worried.

A cold tendril of fear curled round his gut.

"It's Marta. She's disappeared."

CHAPTER 14

*A*my looked around Marta's empty room, her pulse beating erratically. Marta had taken her few belongings...except her Bible. The small Bible Daisy had given her at the shelter, that Amy knew she'd treasured, lay forgotten by the side of her bed. That more than anything told Amy exactly where Marta had gone. With her legs weakening beneath her, she sank onto the bed, hugging her arms around herself.

Following her gaze, Angus picked up the Bible and opened it at the page Marta had dog-eared.

At his sharp intake of breath, Amy looked up. "What is it? Did you find something? Did she leave a note?"

Angus shook his head. "She's marked it at Psalm twenty-seven." His voice was thick with emotion.

Their Psalm. But of course, Marta had read it out that day at the shelter. It had touched her as much as it touched them.

"She's underlined bits. Look." Angus held it out to her.

Amy took the Bible. Marta had underscored some of the

lines in pencil. Running her fingers over the page, she read them aloud, her voice barely a whisper. *"When the wicked advance against me to overpower me, it is my enemies and foes who shall stumble and fall. Though an army besiege me my heart will not fear, though war break out against me, even then I will be confident."* A tear splashed onto the page and it took a moment before she realised it was hers. "Poor Marta," she said softly. "She's been fighting battles this whole time and I never thought about it. We all assumed she was okay."

"It's not your fault," Angus said firmly, taking her hand. "You were always there for her."

"There's always a chance that girls in that situation go back." The house mother stood in the doorway, echoing what she'd told Angus the night before. "And as heartbreaking as it is, you can't force her to leave again until she's ready."

"But we can't just let her go!" Amy exclaimed. "What about Angel? Marta's in danger if she's gone back to that man, and that means Angel is, too."

"I've contacted Social Services," the house mother assured. "Even if she wants to change her mind about the adoption, it's unlikely they'll allow her to keep Angel if she's gone back into an abusive situation. You should still be able to adopt the baby."

"*If* we find her," Angus said glumly.

Amy stared at them both as it dawned upon her that the adoption could be in jeopardy. Until then, she'd just wanted them both to be safe. "We have to find her," she said firmly. "She's in danger. Social Services could take days she might not have. And I don't want to have to take Angel from her forcibly. We have to give her a chance." She looked at Angus and their gazes met and held.

He gave a determined nod. "You're right. Come on." He extended his hand to her.

She rose to her feet, feeling stronger with her hand in his. They would do this together. "Do you have any idea where she might be? Does this Steve have an address?" she asked the house mother.

"I only know he lives somewhere in St. Albans," she replied.

"Not far from the shelter," Amy mused. "Even if Daisy doesn't have an address, someone there might know."

Angus nodded. "She may even have gone to the shelter," he said hopefully, though they both knew the chances of her being with anyone other than Steve were slim.

They got into the car, and as Angus reversed out of the driveway, Amy prayed quietly. "Please, God, guide us to her," she murmured under her breath. "Keep Marta and Angel safe."

Angus reached over and squeezed her knee. "Keep praying, Ames."

She prayed the whole way to the shelter, sometimes silently and sometimes aloud, while Angus kept his eyes resolutely on the road ahead. She'd brought Marta's Bible with her in her bag, and every so often took it out and prayed aloud the lines that Marta had underlined.

She wondered briefly if they were doing the right thing. If Marta had made her decision to return to Steve, what could they do? She'd had her eighteenth birthday a few months ago, and for all intents and purposes was now an adult.

Had she run away because she didn't want to give Angel to her and Angus? Perhaps it was nothing to do with Steve at all. But surely she would have told them? Amy turned her thoughts back to her prayers. If she let panic overtake her, she would go to pieces. She had to hold herself together and focus on finding Marta.

Let her be okay. Let her be safe, she prayed silently. They could sort things out with the adoption later.

When they arrived at the shelter several hours later, they sprinted inside. Sitting at reception, Daisy's eyes widened. "Marta?"

"Yes. Have you seen her?" Hope flared inside Amy momentarily, but was soon crushed when Daisy shook her head. "She left Hope House before six this morning with her things. She's been making secret phone calls...we think she's gone back to Steve," Amy said.

Daisy clasped her hands together and her face went white. "Dear Lord," she whispered.

"Do you know where she might be?" Amy asked.

"I have a prior address for her. I assume it was where she lived with Steve. Whether or not he still lives there is anyone's guess. I'll go and get it." Daisy sprinted to the office while Amy leaned against the counter.

Looking at Angus, her heart ached for him. Dark shadows hung heavily under his eyes and a weary expression filled his face. Underneath, she knew he was panicking even if he wasn't displaying it through his actions.

"We'll find her," she said with more conviction that she felt.

Angus squeezed her hand.

Daisy came out of the office waving a piece of paper in the air.

Angus took it from her. "Thanks, Daisy. Let's go, Amy."

Amy gave her cousin a quick hug, promising to keep her

updated, before following Angus outside. After they jumped into the car, he pulled away with the tyres screeching.

Amy pressed a hand to her stomach, feeling suddenly nauseous. *Dear Lord, please let us be in time.* A horrible premonition that something bad had happened flashed through her mind.

They pulled up outside a block of apartments that had seen better days. The walls were covered in graffiti and rock music boomed from one of the apartments. Somewhere, a dog barked incessantly. It wasn't the type of neighbourhood you'd want your daughter to live in. They went inside and sprinted up the two flights of stairs to the number written on the paper Angus clutched in his hands. A musty smell of stale urine surrounded them.

Amy banged on the door, her breath stuck in her throat. Angus stepped in front of her, ensuring he was between her and whoever opened the door. Amy realised what a risky situation they were potentially putting themselves in.

It doesn't matter. We have to find Marta.

There was no answer. Frustrated, she banged again.

Angus followed suit. "I don't think there's anyone here," he said eventually, sounding deflated.

Amy's shoulders fell.

"They might be out," he said. "We could come back later."

Feeling suddenly dizzy, Amy reached out a hand to steady herself as a wave of nausea swept over her.

"Amy!" Angus put an arm around her.

She stumbled, and for a moment her world went black. An image of Marta curled up in a ball, lying on the floor of a dirty kitchen moved through her mind like a motion picture. "She's inside," she said urgently, straightening as a surge of energy flowed through her. "She's inside that apartment!"

"How do you know?" Angus's brows drew together.

Reaching up, Amy placed her hands on his shoulders and gazed deeply into his eyes. "I have no idea, I just do. Would you believe me if I said God just told me?" She knew she sounded crazy, but Angus looked at her with complete trust.

"Yes. Should we phone the police?" He examined the door. "It doesn't look all that sturdy." Before Amy could stop him or answer, he'd reared back and kicked the door at the lock with all his might.

Amy jumped back but her heart leaped to her throat as the door flew open. "Marta!" she cried, running in behind Angus.

"Here!" he shouted. Amy followed him into the tiny kitchen and then screamed as she saw Marta exactly as she was in her vision. She lay on the floor in a ball, deathly white and still. Kneeling, Amy cradled Marta's head as Angus whipped out his phone and rang for an ambulance.

"There's a pulse, but it's so faint," she cried. A purple bruise spread across the side of Marta's face. A discarded needle lay by her side.

Amy sobbed while holding Marta like a baby. Her gaze was drawn to the red marks in the crook of the girl's arm. She stared at Angus in despair.

He stared back, his face frozen, then crouched down next to them. Together they silently prayed.

It only took a few minutes for the ambulance to arrive, but they were the longest minutes Amy had ever experienced. When she finally heard the sirens, she let out a breath she hadn't known she was holding. She watched helplessly as the paramedics put Marta onto a gurney and carried her downstairs into the ambulance. Wordlessly, she got back into the car with Angus and they followed the ambulance to the hospital.

Marta was rushed inside. They sat in the waiting room for what felt like an age before a female doctor came out to them, her face tight.

Amy's insides flipped. "How is she? And the baby?"

"Are you relatives?" the doctor asked.

Amy and Angus exchanged glances. "We're the baby's adoptive parents," Angus replied.

"How is she?" Amy asked, her heart thumping.

"She overdosed," the doctor said matter-of-factly, "and given her condition, it could have caused damage to the baby. We've stabilised her but she hasn't come around yet. We're going to do an emergency caesarean."

"So, the baby's okay?" Amy asked hopefully, her heart pounding a crescendo.

The doctor grimaced. "There's a heartbeat, but it's faint and erratic. We need to operate immediately. Plus, it's over a month early."

"So, what does that mean?" Angus asked, his voice hoarse.

The doctor visibly swallowed. "It means there's a strong chance the baby won't survive."

CHAPTER 15

*A*my and Angus sat in the small chapel in the hospital's Faith Centre and stared up at the cross, their hands entwined. Amy felt as though her heart had been stolen from her chest only to be replaced by a stone that felt impossibly heavy. The nausea she'd experienced earlier kept returning in waves, and it was almost more than she could bear. She kept trying to pray aloud but could find no words. No words at all. They'd been waiting for news for what seemed forever. Angel had been delivered and was in intensive care, and Marta was still unconscious. That was all they knew.

Next to her, Angus's head was bowed. She took his hand, feeling a small comfort at the warmth of his skin against hers. "They have to be okay, don't they?" she all but pleaded for reassurance.

Angus looked at her bleakly then set his mouth in a determined line. "All we can do is pray. They're in God's hands."

Amy nodded and clasped her other hand over hers and

Angus's entwined ones. She closed her eyes and tried, amidst her pain and fear, to find the still small place in her heart, the place where she would feel God's presence, if she allowed herself to dwell. Whatever happened, she wouldn't again raise the wall she'd built around her heart after the miscarriage.

"God," she said, trying not to choke on a sob. "Please watch over Marta and Angel right now, please enfold them in Your embrace and Your love. Let Angel not only be safe, but let her thrive. Let her know how much she's already loved." Amy paused as emotions welled up, choking her words.

Angus cleared his throat and took over. "Lord God, give us the strength to face whatever may come our way. The strength to support each other, and to support Marta and Angel. You are our stronghold and our fortress, help us to not lose sight of that. Allow us to be strengthened by You and by You alone."

"Please, Lord." Amy's eyes closed as she urgently whispered, "Please send Your healing power to both Marta and Angel. May Your love pierce Marta's darkness and bring her back to wakefulness. May she recover from this overdose and be made whole again. We ask this of You, Lord our God. We ask this of You that Your name might be glorified. Thank You, Lord. Amen." Amy felt strength surge through her as she uttered these words, surrendering all to her Lord and Master.

They sat in silence, and then, despite her fear, deep calm settled over her. A sense of peace and intimacy with the Lord. It was going to be all right, she knew suddenly. One way or the other, it was going to be all right.

"Angus," she said quietly, turning to look at him. "Can we promise each other something?"

"What is it, sweetheart?" He kissed her hand.

"No matter what happens, let's stick together this time. Let's support each other." They'd both made mistakes after the miscarriage, she knew that. This time they needed to be a team.

He slipped his arms around her and gazed at her with eyes filled with love. "I promise. We have a great gift in each other. Let's remember that."

They held hands as they stood. It was time to find out how Marta and Angel were doing. They remained hand in hand as they walked stoically through the hospital corridors to the intensive care ward.

An unfamiliar receptionist sat behind the desk, and when Amy asked about Marta, the young woman looked at her blankly. A cold knot formed in Amy's stomach when the woman checked the system and told them Marta was no longer in the ward.

She looked further and then said, "Oh, she's been moved to the maternity ward. She's in a room by herself, but the baby is with her due to being premature. They're both under observation, but from what I can tell from the notes, it seems they're both coming along. You're welcome to go down."

Weak with relief, Amy burst into tears of joy. "Praise God," she whispered. A wide grin spread across Angus's face and tears sparkled in his eyes. They hugged and held each other tight.

A warm smile tipped the receptionist's lips.

They made their way to the maternity ward, excitement and apprehension fizzing in Amy's stomach. Finally, they were going to meet their baby.

As they found the room and stepped tentatively inside,

Marta looked up with tired eyes. A tiny baby lay in an incubator beside her. Resisting the temptation to run straight to the incubator, Amy approached Marta and took her hand. Stroked it.

"I'm sorry," Marta said weakly.

Amy shook her head, fighting tears. "There's nothing to be sorry about."

"They said you saved me...you came and searched for me," Marta whispered. She gulped. Tears flooded her eyes.

Amy shrugged, not knowing what to say. They'd come to love Marta as if she were family. She *was* family. And they'd do anything to help her. Keep her safe.

As Amy glanced from the new young mother to the beautiful baby in the crib, a new anguish seared her heart. Could Marta truly relinquish the rights to this precious little bundle after everything she'd been through?

CHAPTER 16

*T*hree days later, Amy sat by the side of Marta's bed and watched as the young mother carefully gave Angel a bottle. Marta was not able to breast feed because of the opiates in her system, but other than that, she was much stronger, as was Angel. The pair would be discharged in a few days, all being well.

So far Marta had made no mention of giving Angel to her and Angus and it hung thickly in the air between them. The managers of Hope House had found Marta a place in a three-month rehab facility that was near enough to Salford that they, and Angel, would be able to visit on the weekends. Marta had agreed to go, although the heartbreaking look she'd given Angel had been enough for Amy to know that the young woman didn't want to leave her daughter, now or ever. There was a conversation waiting to be had that Amy didn't know how to broach.

But it was one that needed to be had, and soon. Social

Services were threatening to remove Angel from Marta and place her in foster care unless the adoption papers were signed. Marta's relapse and the fact that she'd returned to an abusive partner meant she was considered high risk. Amy wanted to scream at the injustice of it all. If the system hadn't failed Marta, she would never have ended up in the situation she was in. Amy thanked God for bringing them together in the first place, for making beauty from ashes. But now, this was an almost impossible situation.

Marta burped Angel then passed her to Amy. Amy took the tiny bundle gratefully, breathing in the smell of her. She stared at the little girl's sweet face and thanked God again that she and her mother had survived.

Then she looked at Marta and saw the way she was still gazing at Angel. Amy took a deep breath, asked God for guidance, and said softly, "Marta, are you still okay with the adoption going ahead? We need to get things finalised before you go to the rehab centre."

Marta flinched, then, with her jaw rigid, said in a determined voice, "Yes, let's get the paperwork done today."

"Is it still what you want?" As Amy searched the girl's eyes, they flooded with tears. Amy felt her heart would break. She knew beyond all doubt she couldn't take a baby from a mother who loved it. But what choice was there? If Angel didn't go to her and Angus, she would go to some other couple.

"I didn't know," Marta said in a voice that was all but a whisper, "that I would love her so much. To think that I nearly..." Her voice hitched as tears splashed onto her cheeks.

Amy swallowed hard to stop her own tears from falling. "Don't blame yourself, Marta. Please. You were vulnerable. We should have seen you were struggling and offered you more support."

Marta shook her head and brushed her cheeks. "There was nothing you could have done. It was like something got in my head again. I kept thinking about how I was going to be alone. That I wouldn't have anyone after...after..."

"After we adopted Angel." Amy completed the sentence for her.

Marta bit her lip. "It was selfish. I know that. But this dark cloud descended upon me and I couldn't see my way through, even when I tried to pray. I kept thinking how Steve was the only family I had, no matter how bad he was...so I gave in and phoned him. He sounded like he'd changed. He said he wanted to be a good father...then he turned on me almost as soon as I arrived."

She had to take a breath. Amy could only imagine the horror poor Marta had faced. She'd given her statement to the police and Steve had been arrested and charged. A restraining order had been taken out to prevent him from coming near Marta or Angel while he was on bail, but none of that would compensate for the abuse she'd suffered at his hands.

"Social Services won't let me keep her now, anyway," Marta said sadly, "and that's my own fault. But I'd never go back again. He could have killed Angel..." She broke off and shuddered, then stared at Amy with wide eyes. "You have to take her, or she'll go into care. Steve could even make a claim for her."

"I'm praying that Steve will be in prison," Amy said firmly, "but yes, of course we would never let that happen to her or you." She peered at the beautiful bundle in her arms, sleeping contentedly. Joy and sorrow ebbed and flowed through her body one after the other. She loved Angel, but she loved Marta, too. And Marta was Angel's mother. She had to do what the Spirit was prompting. The right thing…

"Marta," Amy began, taking a deep breath, "how about we apply to foster Angel for a while? While you're in rehab and get on your feet? Then we can make a decision about adoption depending on what you want to do."

Marta's eyes grew large. "I…I don't know," she stammered, clearly overwhelmed. She stared at Angel. "I want to be her mother," she whispered, "but I don't know how."

Amy placed the baby back in Marta's arms, feeling as if her heart would break at the way Marta clutched her daughter to her chest as if she never wanted to let her go. "You simply love her," Amy whispered as she leaned down and kissed the top of Angel's soft, downy head. She nodded at Angus, and the two of them left to allow Marta precious time with her baby and to ponder her future.

THREE DAYS LATER, Amy sat on the back verandah with Angus, her head resting on his shoulder as they watched the sun sink slowly in the west, filling the sky with hues of pinks and oranges. God's canvas. She smiled at her husband, her heart bursting with love.

On the chair next to them sat the baby monitor, picking up every little snuffle that Angel made as she slept in her bassinet, safe and secure. Given her start in life, she was an absolute miracle. If they had to hand her over to Marta it would be the most difficult thing they would ever have to do. But Amy also knew in her heart that she could not take Marta's chance to be a mother from her. Of course, it all depended on Marta remaining stable, but Amy had faith in her.

Earlier, they'd dropped Marta at Hope House from where she would be taken to the rehab facility. It would be two weeks before they were allowed to visit. Amy had watched with anguish as Marta showered Angel with kisses before handing her to Amy.

"Phone as soon as you can," Amy had told her, hugging the girl tightly.

"I will." Marta sniffed. "Will you pray for me?"

"Every day," Amy whispered. Both their faces were damp with tears. Even Angus had tears in his eyes. This was hard for him, too. It was hard for them all. But they would get through it by keeping their eyes and hearts on the Lord.

"I'm proud of you," Angus said, slipping his arm around her after Marta walked away. "It's a brave thing to do, relinquishing your chance to be a mother."

"Our chance to be parents," Amy said sadly, turning to him. "But you know, after everything that's happened, I believe that God brought us all together for a reason. Whether that was to adopt Angel or just care for her while Marta gets herself on track, I believe it will all work out according to His plan. I can't think about what I want anymore. It's what's best for Angel."

"And that's why I'm proud of you. The faith and compassion you've shown throughout this...I'm truly in awe of you, my love."

She looked deep into his eyes. "But what about you? I know how much you want to be a father."

He nodded, tucking a loose strand of hair behind her ear. "I do. But if it's not God's plan for us? I have you, Amy, and our marriage is more than enough for me."

Tears trembled on her eyelids. He was right. In all their striving to have a baby, they had once nearly lost the simple joy of having each other. This last year, as difficult as it had been, had brought them so much closer, and Amy knew that while she may always carry a certain sadness at not having their own children, she was also incredibly blessed. She leaned in to kiss Angus, then groaned as a wave of nausea swept over her.

"What's wrong?" he asked, his brow creased with concern.

Leaning back in her chair, Amy pressed a hand to her stomach. "I feel sick all the time. At first, I thought it was stress, but it's not passing. If anything, it's getting worse. And I'm so hungry. I'll go to the doctor tomorrow and see if I've got some kind of virus."

Angus's eyes grew large.

"What is it?" she asked.

"Sweetheart," he said slowly, "you were like this before...when you were pregnant."

"Don't be silly." She laughed, but then stopped as realisation dawned. Because of all the drama, she hadn't even thought about it, but she was two weeks late. She shook her head. "No, it can't be," she said, even as she wondered if it could be possible. But no, she couldn't dare think it, only to be wrong.

In a daze, she stood and walked upstairs to the bathroom. At the back of the cupboard was an unused test kit from when they'd been trying for a baby. Rifling through toiletries, she found it, her hand shaking.

A few minutes later, she stared at two thin blue lines.

She was pregnant.

EPILOGUE

$\mathcal{A}$ ngus stood proudly over his son's hospital crib, staring at the most amazing being in God's creation. His son. Archie. *His son.* He still couldn't quite believe it was true. The last seven and a half months had been a time of much joy, but also worry, as he and Amy had spent the first few months with bated breath, knowing the possibility was high that Amy would miscarry again. Prayer, their love for each other, and faith in God had kept them grounded, not to mention caring for Angel at the same time. It had been an absolute whirlwind. As the pregnancy had progressed and later scans had confirmed Archie was safe and well, they had allowed themselves to make plans and accept the idea that they were finally going to be parents. God was good, Angus thought with a grin. Looking down at Archie, he was unable to keep the smile from his face.

A murmur came from the bed and he glanced over at Amy

who was just waking from sleep. She smiled then her gaze went straight to Archie.

"He's sleeping," Angus told her. Amy smiled a wide, contented smile and reached out a hand for him. Angus took it and sat in the chair next to her. She looked radiant but tired. Not surprising, given her labour had lasted most of the day. And the midwife had told him that was short. Angus had found himself absolutely blown away by the birth and the raw, primal beauty of it. Watching Archie take his first breath as he was laid on Amy's breast had filled him to bursting with gratitude and love for God and His incredible creation. He had also fallen in love even more deeply with his wife, something he wouldn't have thought possible.

They gazed at each other, lost in their contentment, then heard voices outside the door.

"Aunty Amy!" Will and Lucy ran in, followed by Fleur who was holding a bunch of flowers. She let out a gasp of delight at the sight of baby Archie in his crib, then handed the flowers to Angus before leaning down and embracing Amy tenderly. "Congratulations, sweetheart. Well done," Fleur whispered to her as Angus placed the flowers in the water jug in lieu of a vase.

Behind them, Callum stepped in grinning. He kissed Amy and slapped Angus on the back. Then Marta followed with Angel in her arms, her face practically splitting, her smile was so wide. She passed the dark-haired baby girl to Fleur and leaned down to give Amy a long, long hug.

Angus looked on, marvelling at how everything had turned out. Marta had completed rehab and had moved back to Hope House with Angel before being recently housed in her own apartment. Angel was now fully in her care, although Marta received support from a social worker as well as continuing support from Hope House. She was returning to college as soon as Angel turned one, and she was heavily involved at church. She was doing well, although she was still processing her traumas and knew it was important to take things a day at a time. She and Amy were incredibly close, and he and Amy had been made godparents at Angel's recent dedication ceremony. Suddenly they had a bigger family than they had ever planned.

Perching on the end of the bed, he watched his family and friends and thought once again how good God was. "Guys," he said, cutting through all the excited chatter, "I think this would be a really good time to pray together."

Everyone nodded, and they held hands around the bed. Callum, as the pastor in the room, began the prayer. "Lord, we thank You for the blessings You've poured out upon us all, and especially this day for the blessing of baby Archie. For seeing Amy safe through the birth and giving her and Angus the gift of parenthood after all they've been through. You have done great things in their lives and we honour You."

Marta, her voice strong and clear, went next. "Lord, I can never fully thank You enough for Amy and Angus and for everything they've done for me and Angel. Thank You for little Archie who couldn't ask for better parents."

"Lord, we pray for a swift recovery for Amy from the birth," Fleur said in her soft voice, "and we pray Your blessing over this family. Keep them safe in Your loving embrace and walk with them through their new journey."

Angus hesitated. He looked at Amy, squeezed her hand, and

said simply, "We thank You for our son, Lord. We thank You for Archie."

"Amen," they all chorused, and right on cue the tiny, healthy baby boy released a thin, hungry wail. Angus picked him up and laid him in Amy's arms, then went out with Callum to find the nurse with the tea trolley so as to give Amy privacy while she fed their son.

Angus felt utterly gratified. Yes, he was sure this new journey would have its ups and downs, but right now, he couldn't be happier. He and Amy had held on to their love for one another through the trials and tribulations and had been rewarded for their faith. They'd turned their hearts and faces to the Lord and sought Him, and He had blessed them beyond measure.

Sometimes, Angus thought, dreams really did come true.

The Lord is my light and my salvation—whom shall I fear? The Lord is the stronghold of my life—of whom shall I be afraid? When the wicked advance against me to devour me, it is my enemies and my foes that will stumble and fall. Though an army besiege me, my heart will not fear; though war break out against me, even then I will be confident. One thing I ask from the Lord, this only do I seek: that I may dwell in the house of the Lord all the days of my life, to gaze on the beauty of the Lord and to seek Him in His temple. For in the day of trouble He will keep me safe in His dwelling; He will hide me in the shelter of His sacred tent and set me high upon a rock. Then my head will be exalted above the enemies who surround me; at His sacred tent I will sacrifice with shouts of joy; I will sing and make music to the Lord. Hear my voice when I call, Lord; be merciful to me and answer me. My heart says of You "Seek His face!" Your face, Lord, I will seek. Do not hide Your face from me, do not turn Your servant away in anger; You have been my helper. Do not reject me or forsake me, God my Saviour. Though my father and mother forsake me, the Lord will receive me. Teach me Your way, Lord; lead me in a straight path because of my oppressors. Do not turn me over to the desire of my foes, for false witnesses rise up against me, spouting malicious accusations. I remain confident of this: I will see the goodness of the Lord in the land of the living. Wait for the Lord; be strong and take heart and wait for the Lord.'

Psalm 27

NOTE FROM THE AUTHOR

I hope you enjoyed "Because We Dreamed", and that the message of Psalm 27 touched your heart. If you'd like to follow Marta's story, "Because We Believed", the 4th book in the "Transformed by Love Christian Romance Series", will be available soon. To make sure you don't miss it and to be notified of all my new releases, why not join my Readers' list? You'll also receive a free thank-you copy of "Hank and Sarah - A Love Story", a clean love story with God at the center. http://www.julietteduncan.com/linkspage/282748

Enjoyed "Because We Dreamed"? You can make a big difference. Help other people find this book by writing a review and telling them why you liked it. Honest reviews of my books help bring them to the attention of other readers just like yourself, and I'd be very grateful if you could spare just five minutes to leave a review (it can be as short as you like) on the book's Amazon page.

Keep reading for a bonus chapter of "Her Kind-Hearted Billionaire". I think you'll enjoy it.

Blessings,

Juliette

Chapter 1

Sydney, Australia

Nicholas Barrington sat behind his desk on the forty-fifth floor of the tower bearing his family's name and removed his pre-prepared meal from his lunch bag. Below, Sydney Harbour shimmered in the midday sun and looked spectacular. A small tugboat, looking much like a toy from this height, guided a large cruise ship through the harbour towards the heads, while a number of yachts sliced through the water easily in what Nick assumed was a strong breeze, given the trim of their sails. The problem was, being on the forty-fifth floor, he was removed from reality. The view was sensational, but he felt like a spectator. He'd much rather be a participant.

A firm knock sounded on his office door, pulling his gaze from the vista. Nicholas swivelled around. Alden, his brother and fellow director, sauntered in and sank into the chair on the opposite side of the desk. "Taking time for lunch today, bro?" At thirty-one, Alden was two years younger than Nicholas and had the same sea-blue eyes, although his hair was lighter.

"Yes. I was just about to eat. Did you bring yours?" For a moment, Nicholas forgot he was talking with his brother. Of course Alden hadn't brought his lunch.

Alden scoffed, eyeing Nicholas's bag with amusement. "It'll be here in five minutes."

Nicholas pulled out his sandwich and salad, glad he didn't have to wait for his meal to be delivered.

"Eating in here today?" Charity, their younger sister, appeared in the doorway. The sharp bob framing her pixie-like face was the same dark colour as his, but she had their late mother's emerald green eyes. She plopped onto the chair next to Alden and pulled a portable blender filled with green powder from her carry bag. Opening a bottle of water, she poured half of it in and hit the button.

"That looks disgusting," Nicholas shouted over the whir of the machine.

"Try some if you like."

Grimacing, he quickly shook his head. "No thanks. I'll stick to my sandwich."

Moments later, a young man knocked tentatively on the door holding a rectangular food box. Alden waved him in and took the box.

Setting it on the desk, he peeled back the cardboard lid, revealing a large steak with new potatoes and green beans. Although it smelled appetising, as Nicholas took the last bite of his sandwich and moved onto the salad, he was thankful his tastes weren't the same as his siblings. He was a simple man with simple needs.

"It's all right, but it could be better," Alden commented after swallowing his first mouthful.

Nicholas ignored his brother's comment and instead focused on Charity who'd just turned the blender off. The silence was very welcome.

"So, you know I was meant to be flying to Bali tomorrow for that meditation retreat?" Angling her head, she glanced at him as she poured some of the green concoction into a glass.

He nodded. Of late, Charity had been delving into meditation and something about self-praise and how to be her own deity. Not what Nicholas would have considered a worthwhile venture, but, each to his own. He'd started exploring things of a spiritual nature as well, but his initial explorations had led him to a traditional church, although he hadn't yet made up his mind whether that was what he wanted.

"Looks like I'll have to postpone the flight to another day." Charity released a frustrated sigh before taking a mouthful of what Nicholas considered a disgusting looking green concoction.

"Why's that?"

"Why?" Charity's green eyes bulged. "Because of that lazy pilot." Her voice rose to a crescendo and Nicholas wouldn't have been surprised if the whole floor had heard.

"Ugh, don't even get me started." Alden shook his head, waving a fork in the air.

Charity leaned forward. "Can you believe he told me he can't work tomorrow? I mean, I'm his boss. It's not like we're ordering him to fly every day. He gets plenty of time off. I just needed him for one day."

"Why can't he take you?" Nicholas asked in a calm voice.

"His daughter's having surgery. I get that family is important and all that, but honestly, it's only a few hours each way. He'd be back before she even woke up."

Nicholas studied his sister with sadness. He doubted she knew that Roger's small daughter had been born with special needs and her surgeries required extensive preparation. Even the anesthesia was a risk. But it was no use saying anything. She wouldn't understand or care. "Did he suggest anyone else who could step in?"

"I don't want anyone else. They wouldn't know our plane like he does." Charity blew out another breath and sipped her concoction. "Anyway, I think we should fire him." Shifting in her chair, she crossed her long, slim legs and adjusted her skirt.

"I agree," Alden said. "Last time he took me to Dubai, we were an hour late. He said it was because they didn't have a place for us to land, but isn't it his job to make sure all of that's figured out ahead of time?"

Nicholas sighed. "That's hardly his fault. Sometimes unexpected things happen that are out of anyone's control. You know Roger's competent and he always does his best."

"You're so naive, big brother. You always want to see the good in everybody. No wonder they take advantage of you." Alden gave him a withering look.

Nicholas pursed his lips. He wished his siblings could show a little more humility and understanding, especially since they'd been given so much. How could they be so cruel and selfish when it came to others?

Taking a sip from his water bottle, Nicholas shut out his siblings as they continued talking about things he couldn't relate to. Although the three were very different, it saddened him they weren't closer. Without any other family, they only had each other. But all they ever talked about was the business and what gave them pleasure, like Charity's Bali trip. Beyond that, very little of depth ever entered their conversations. While the two continued to talk about things of no interest to him, Nicholas returned to his work, but his ears pricked when Alden mentioned their late grandfather, James Barrington.

"You know, old James wouldn't have liked us wasting the money on a lousy staffer. Just because a man's nice enough doesn't make him worth the money." It seemed they'd returned to the issue of whether to fire Roger or not. Nicholas groaned. From what he remembered of James Barrington, firing a man because of an important family issue would have been the last thing he would have done.

When he died, the three siblings had inherited their grandfather's fortune, amassed during the mining boom of the eighties. A billion for each, plus the company divided between them. Now the trio lacked for nothing, but as much as Nicholas appreciated the life he now had, he would much have preferred his grandfather, and his parents, to still be alive. How different things would have been if his parents had inherited instead of the three grandchildren.

He sighed sadly. Yes, he'd give just about anything to have his parents back. It didn't seem fair that their lives had been snuffed out while they were still in their prime.

"So, do you think we should fire him? After he takes me to Bali, of course?" Charity asked nonchalantly, inspecting her perfectly manicured nails.

"Don't be a fool," Alden said harshly.

For a moment, Nicholas held hopes that his brother might stick up for the man, but they were soon dashed when Alden continued. "You should probably wait until he brings you back from Bali. You don't want to be stuck there!" He laughed, and Charity joined in.

Nicholas seethed. He had to say something, but he needed to remain calm and rational. An emotional defense of the pilot wouldn't go over well with his siblings. "Why don't we give him another chance? His daughter is having surgery, it's hardly a time to be selfish."

Charity huffed with exasperation. "Whatever you say, big brother. Although I don't see how it affects you, since you never use the private jet, anyway." Her voice dripped with sarcasm.

Biting his lip, Nicholas brushed her comments and attitude off. They'd soon forget about the pilot and move on to a discussion about shoes or something as equally trivial.

"Well, I'm headed out. I've got a hot yoga class this afternoon." Charity stood, tossed her rubbish in the bin, and then picked up her blender.

"Don't you need more than that shake before working out?" Alden waved the last piece of steak on his fork as if he were teasing her with it.

She rolled her eyes. "Keep your cow, thanks." With that, she turned and left the room, teetering on her stilettos.

Alden mopped up the last of his gravy, said a brief goodbye to Nicholas, and then also left the office.

Leaning back in his chair, Nicholas released a slow breath and gazed out the window. The cruise ship was long gone, but a Manly ferry was approaching Circular Quay, leaving white frothy water in its wake.

As much as he loved his siblings, he also loved his peace

and quiet. He sometimes wondered about their grandfather and whether he'd be pleased with how his grandchildren were handling his fortune. James Barrington was renowned for his kindness, a rarity in the ruthless mining industry, and Nicholas wished he'd gotten to know him better before he passed. He sensed he could have learned a lot from him, and not just about the business. He'd heard that James Barrington was a religious man. Another rarity in the industry.

Swivelling his chair all the way around, Nicholas set back to work, tapping his fingers on the keyboard, opening emails from clients, studying spreadsheets. Millions of dollars in transactions and exchanges occurred on a weekly basis and the company was doing well, but as Managing Director, he needed to stay on top of it.

Their clients were happy, and he had reason to be proud of the company that he and his siblings had maintained and grown since taking over almost ten years ago. To the world at large, they were a success.

But sometimes, in the still of night, when he had time to think, he pondered what success really was. What was he missing by spending all his days on the forty-fifth floor?

Grab your copy of *Her Kind-Hearted Billionaire*.

OTHER BOOKS BY JULIETTE DUNCAN

Find all of Juliette Duncan's books on her website:
www.julietteduncan.com/library

Transformed by Love Christian Romance Series

Book 1 - *Because We Loved*

A decorated Lieutenant Colonel plagued with guilt. A captivating widow whose husband was killed under his watch…

Book 2 - *Because We Forgave*

A fallen TV personality hiding from his failures. An ex-wife and family facing their fears…

Book 3 - *Because We Dreamed*

When dreams are shattered, can hope be restored?

Billionaires with Heart Christian Romance Series

Her Kind-Hearted Billionaire

A reluctant billionaire, a grieving young woman, and the trip that changes their lives forever...

Her Generous Billionaire

A grieving billionaire, a solo mother, and a woman determined to sabotage their relationship...

Her Disgraced Billionaire

A billionaire in jail, a nurse who cares, and the challenge that changes their lives forever...

"The Billionaires with Heart Christian Romance Series" is a series of stand-alone books that are both God honoring and entertaining. Get your copy now,

enjoy and be blessed!

A Time for Everything Series

A Time For Everything Series is a mature-age contemporary Christian romance series set in Sydney, Australia and Texas, USA. If you like real-life characters, faith-filled families, and friendships that become something more, then you'll love these inspirational second-chance romances.

The True Love Series

Set in Australia, what starts out as simple love story grows into a family saga, including a dad battling bouts of depression and guilt, an ex-wife with issues of her own, and a young step-mum trying to mother a teenager who's confused and hurting. Through it all, a love story is woven. A love story between a caring God and His precious children as He gently draws them to Himself and walks with them through the trials and joys of life.

"A beautiful Christian story. I enjoyed all of the books in this series. They all brought out Christian concepts of faith in action."

"Wonderful set of books. Weaving the books from story to story. Family living, God, & learning to trust Him with all their hearts."

The Precious Love Series

The Precious Love Series continues the story of Ben, Tessa and Jayden from the The True Love Series, although each book can be read on its own. All of the books in this series will warm your heart and draw you closer to the God who loves and cherishes you without condition.

"I loved all the books by Juliette, but those about Jaydon and Angie's stories are my favorites...can't wait for the next one..."

"Juliette Duncan has earned my highest respect as a Christian romance writer. She continues to write such touching stories about real life and the tragedies, turmoils, and joys that happen while we are living. The words that she uses to write about her characters relationships with God can only come from someone that has had a very close & special with her Lord and Savior herself. I have read all of her books and if you are a reader of Christian fiction books I would highly recommend her books." Vicki

The Shadows Series

An inspirational romance, a story of passion and love, and of God's

inexplicable desire to free people from pasts that haunt them so they can live a life full of His peace, love and forgiveness, regardless of the circumstances. Book 1, *"Lingering Shadows"* is set in England, and follows the story of Lizzy, a headstrong, impulsive young lady from a privileged background, and Daniel, a roguish Irishman who sweeps her off her feet. But can Lizzy leave the shadows of her past behind and give Daniel the love he deserves, and will Daniel find freedom and release in God?

Hank and Sarah - A Love Story, *the Prequel to "The Madeleine Richards Series" is a FREE thank you gift for joining my mailing list. You'll also be the first to hear about my next books and get exclusive sneak previews. Get your free copy at www.julietteduncan.com/subscribe*

The Madeleine Richards Series

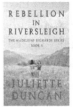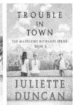

Although the 3 book series is intended mainly for pre-teen/ Middle Grade girls, it's been read and enjoyed by people of all ages.

"Juliette has a fabulous way of bringing her characters to life. Maddy is at typical teenager with authentic views and actions that truly make it feel like you are feeling her pain and angst. You want to enter into her situation and make everything better. Mom and soon to be dad respond to her with love and gentle persuasion while maintaining their faith and trust in Jesus, whom they know, will give them wisdom as they continue on their lives journey. Appropriate for teenage readers but any age can enjoy." Amazon Reader

The Potter's House Books...stories of hope, redemption, and second chances. Find out more here:

http://pottershousebooks.com/our-books/

The Homecoming

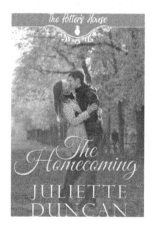

Kayla McCormack is a famous pop-star, but her life is a mess. Dane Carmichael has a disability, but he has a heart for God. He had a crush on her at school, but she doesn't remember him. His simple faith and life fascinate her, but can she surrender her life of fame and fortune to find true love?

Unchained

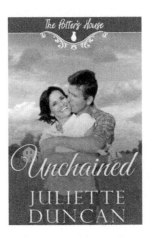

Imprisoned by greed – redeemed by love

Sally Richardson has it all. A devout, hard-working, well-respected husband, two great kids, a beautiful home, wonderful friends. Her life is perfect. Until it isn't.

When Brad Richardson, accountant, business owner, and respected church member, is sentenced to five years in jail, Sally is shell-shocked. How had she not known about her husband's fraudulent activity? And how, as an upstanding member of their tight-knit community, did he ever think he'd get away with it? He's defrauded clients, friends, and fellow church members. She doubts she can ever trust him again.

Locked up with murderers and armed robbers, Brad knows that the only way to survive his incarceration is to seek God with all his heart - something he should have done years ago. But how does he convince his family that his remorse is genuine? Will they ever forgive him?

He's failed them. But most of all, he's failed God. His poor decisions have ruined this once perfect family.

They've lost everything they once held dear. Will they lose each other as well?

Blessings of Love

She's going on mission to help others. He's going to win her heart.

Skye Matthews, bright, bubbly and a committed social work major, is the pastor's daughter. She's in love with Scott Anderson, the most eligible bachelor, not just at church, but in the entire town.

Scott lavishes her with flowers and jewellery and treats her like a lady, and Skye has no doubt that life with him would be amazing. And yet, sometimes, she can't help but feel he isn't committed enough. Not to her, but to God.

She knows how important Scott's work is to him, but she has a niggling feeling that he isn't prioritising his faith, and that concerns her. If only he'd join her on the mission trip to Burkina Faso…

Scott Anderson, a smart, handsome civil engineering graduate, has just received the promotion he's been working for for months. At age twenty-four, he's the youngest employee to ever hold a position of this calibre, and he's pumped.

Scott has been dating Skye long enough to know that she's 'the one', but just when he's about to propose, she asks him to go on mission with her. His plans of marrying her are thrown to the wind.

Can he jeopardise his career to go somewhere he's never heard of, to work amongst people he'd normally ignore?

If it's the only way to get a ring on Skye's finger, he might just risk it...

And can Skye's faith last the distance when she's confronted with a truth she never expected?

Stand Alone Christian Romantic Suspense

Leave Before He Kills You

When his face grew angry, I knew he could murder...

That face drove me and my three young daughters to flee across Australia.

I doubted he'd ever touch the girls, but if I wanted to live and see them grow, I had to do something.

The plan my friend had proposed was daring and bold, but it also gave me hope.

My heart thumped. What if he followed?

Radical, honest and real, this Christian romantic suspense is one woman's journey to freedom you won't put down…get your copy and read it now.

ABOUT THE AUTHOR

Juliette Duncan is a Christian fiction author, passionate about writing stories that will touch her readers' hearts and make a difference in their lives. Although a trained school teacher, Juliette spent many years working alongside her husband in their own business, but is now relishing the opportunity to follow her passion for writing stories she herself would love to read. Based in Brisbane, Australia, Juliette and her husband have five adult children, eight grandchildren, and an elderly long haired dachshund. Apart from writing, Juliette loves exploring the great world we live in, and has travelled extensively, both within Australia and overseas. She also enjoys social dancing and eating out.

Connect with Juliette:

Email: juliette@julietteduncan.com

Website: www.julietteduncan.com

Facebook: www.facebook.com/JulietteDuncanAuthor

Twitter: https://twitter.com/Juliette_Duncan

Made in the USA
Monee, IL
21 November 2019